IN A ROUGH AND TUMBLE GALAXY,

*Ruled by gun and muscle...
When you need the very best mercenary, bounty hunter, bodyguard or just straight muscle, you find a ...*

Human for Hire.

Please note:
No actual aliens were harmed during the writing of this book.

1

The Human glanced down at the ground two hundred ten stories below and felt his stomach tighten. He was attached to the outside of a large, plate glass window by electronic suction pads on his knees and with another pad connected to his chest harness, keeping him from toppling over backward. As he looked down at the ground forty-two hundred feet below, he wondered if this was such a good idea, especially when the trickiest part of the operation was still to come.

Now, Adam Cain looked up at the connecting skyway between the twin three-hundred-story buildings. It was still five stories farther up and two hundred feet long and was where Adam had his grappling gun aimed ... for the second time. He'd already shot one dart at the underside of the aerial causeway and missed when a stiff wind came whistling between the structures and knocked it off course.

Fortunately, he brought a spare ... but only one. After discarding the useless lead cord, he replaced it with another. A new launching charge was then inserted into the gun, and now, he twisted around, taking aim at the target ... again.

He pulled the trigger, and the dart shot off, this time striking the bottom of the concourse about two-thirds along the length of the tunnel. It made contact and stuck. The dart was fitted with an electronic suction pad of its own, and now Adam tugged on the line, making sure it had a good purchase. The line felt firm in his hand.

Even so, Adam was taking a chance that the pad would hold his weight. He hooked the carabiner clip to his chest harness and then readied himself.

"Okay, let's do this thing," he said aloud to his Artificial Telepathy Device—his ATD—even though he didn't need to. They were linking mentally, but hearing his own voice over the whistling wind was comforting, as much as anything could be comforting in a situation like this. "On my mark, release the suction."

I am ready, Adam, said Charlie, the voice of his ATD sounding in his mind. *A reminder: You must contact the window squarely with at least one pad so I can get a secure lock. If you hit it at an angle, the pad will not adhere.*

"I got it. Okay, get ready. On my mark ... three, two, one ... mark!"

Through the AI's link with the electronic controls of the pads, Charlie released the suction, sending Adam swinging out across the open space between the buildings. His pivot line was about thirty feet beyond the center of the concourse, which meant he should have enough natural momentum to reach the other side. The problem: when he was released from the window, he had his back to the other building and with the suction cups located on the front side of his knees and palms. Now, Adam had to twist his body in mid-flight, bringing his knees to bear on the rapidly approaching wall of dark glass. And he almost made it.

His right knee slammed into a window but at an odd angle. Charlie activated the suction, and there was a momentary lurch as Adam's body hung motionless for a split second before ricocheting off the glass. In desperation, he reached out with his right hand, placing the palm against the window with his arm fully extended. The pad on his hand let out a loud sucking sound before quickly falling silent, the connection made and secure.

Adam now hung in the air, his chest harness connected to the concourse high above and at an angle, and with his right arm stuck to the building. His body weight and the angle of the supporting cord from above were pulling his body in two directions, with the distinct possibility that it could break the seal on his right hand.

"Release the upper suction pad!" Adam called out to Charlie. The AI obliged, and the dart released itself from the bottom of the concourse. With the pressure on the cord removed, Adam dropped down a couple of feet, and his body slammed against the glass, his back hitting first and twisting his right arm at a painful angle. He now hung two hundred ten stories above the ground, suspended by one twisted arm and a single suction pad.

Feeling behind him, he pushed off with his feet so he could twist around and face the wall of glass. He angled his knees up and made contact with the glass. Instantly, the suction was applied. Then, with his free left hand, he took the chest suction pad and stuck it to the glass. Charlie released his right hand, allowing Adam to unwind his arm with a painful grimace.

His continually-circulating cloning juice—being both a benefit and a curse—kept the pain in his right shoulder down to only a dull throb. The problem with not feeling pain as much as he used to was he often wasn't aware of how badly he was injured. He was fairly sure his shoulder was dislocated, but at the moment, he didn't know how much it would hinder his mission. He would heal remarkably fast, but it wasn't instantaneous.

Adam worked his shoulder, feeling the dislocation with his left hand. It was there; the joint didn't feel right. He placed his right arm across his chest and then yanked quickly with his left, hearing the joint pop back into place. He grimaced slightly, more a sympathy reaction than from any real pain. That should hold it for a while, at least long enough to complete his mission.

Next, Adam considered where he was. There was still an inch-thick layer of reinforced tempered glass he had to get through before he could enter the building. Alternately releasing and then activating the suction pads, Adam moved sideways toward the mullion between the windows. With his body held firmly against one pane of glass, Adam set to work preparing the other pane for the surgical operation he was about to perform, placing industrial strength tape on the glass at strategic points. Then he took out a laser knife and began cutting.

Soon, Adam had a three-foot-square section cut on the glass, which was held in place by the tape. He was positioned at floor level of the office on the other side of the window, and as he pressed inward, the cut panel fell to the carpeted floor, muffling the sound.

From the schematics, Adam knew this room was a secretarial pool, and at this late hour, it was unoccupied. Now, he twisted his body so he could place his head and torso through the opening before releasing the knee suction cups, allowing him to slide inside completely.

He lay on the soft carpet for a few moments, not because he was tired, but just to get a sense of where he was. It was better here than hanging four thousand feet up on the side of a building over a mile high. *Damn alien technology*, he thought. Structures didn't need to be this high, and especially two of them side by side and joined by twenty skyway concourses. But that's how they did it in the city of Halmon on the planet of Calinan. It would have been simpler if the bad guys hung out in a warehouse on the seedier side of town. Instead, they occupied half of the South Tower, and with multiple layers of security beginning at ground level and growing tighter the higher one went in the building.

That was why *The Human* had decided to bypass all the checkpoints and take the Tarzan approach, swinging across the gap between the Towers. Adam had to admit he'd always wanted to try something like this since watching Tom Cruise hang off the side of the Burj Khalifa building in the movie *Ghost Protocol*. Anything Tom could do; Adam Cain could do better. And for real.

He chuckled to himself, prompting a response from Charlie.

Is there something funny I should be aware of? the A.I. asked in his mind. Although Adam and Charlie could speak telepathically, Charlie couldn't read his thoughts … not unless Adam let him.

Not funny, just nostalgic, Adam thought to the A.I.

Fantasizing about Tom Cruise again? Charlie asked.

Don't make it weird, Adam answered. *It's more out of professional respect than anything else.*

Charlie let the subject drop.

I am detecting one hundred ninety-six energy weapons in the upper part of the building, the A.I. reported, sobering Adam and focusing his attention once again on the mission.

That many, at this hour?

It does seem excessive, Charlie confirmed. *However, it is a large building with a lot of Sylos Syndicate members present.*

And this isn't even their main headquarters; it's just a satellite operation, Adam added.

You did choose a difficult task for us to achieve, Charlie said. *Three individuals wanted by Unidor Security. Not even fugitives, just suspected criminals.*

Hey, it pays really well, Adam reminded his ATD.

Of which I have no feelings either way since I cannot share in any of it.

Adam grimaced. *Charlie, I think you're becoming a little too sentient. You almost sound jealous.*

You do realize that it is my existence—as well as your own—that you risk each time you go on a mission such as this.

Adam frowned. *I didn't know you felt that way.*

My programming has changed recently—

Since you became a father?

I can trace the change to around that time, Charlie admitted unabashedly.

Adam was still trying to wrap his mind around the fact that Charlie—his ATD—and his spaceship's internal A.I. system—Beth—had developed a program together, a program they christened David, ostensibly named after Adam's long-deceased father. The idea of computers writing computer programs wasn't unique, but the way these two reacted was as if they had real feelings toward their collaborative program. They had each contributed a part of themselves to David's creation and, as such, felt a bond not only to the program but to each other as well.

And now Charlie was considering his own mortality. If Adam died—again—then Charlie would die, too. And where would that leave Beth and Lil' Davy? Adam wondered if Charlie had a life insurance policy. It might be a good idea...

Adam shouldn't be having thoughts like this, not at this moment. It was hard enough pushing himself to take the risks he did. But Charlie was right; he didn't need to take this assignment. Nor did he have to play Tarzan to get here. And the money—although substantial—wasn't his main driving force. What was it then? The challenge? The thrill? The death wish?

Adam Cain would have to think on that for a while, and with a deeper introspection than he'd been doing lately. He did seem to be spiraling toward something. But what?

Then Adam snorted and got to his feet. This was neither the time nor the place to be having these thoughts. He'd made it this far. He still needed to find the criminals, place them under arrest and then get them out of the building with himself—and Charlie—included. And that last part he was still a little unclear—the part about how he would get them out of the building.

Earlier in the day, Adam had watched from a secure location as the three suspects arrived at the building. He had Charlie fly near-microscopic drones up to them and then embed the trackers in their clothing. Now, Charlie projected a heads-up display before his eyes, showing the locations of his ... his suspects. Normally, Adam would be referring to them as his bounties, but that wasn't right in this case. The three aliens hadn't been found guilty of a crime … not yet. Still, Unidor issued an arrest warrant for them, with a tidy little sum of two hundred fifty-thousand energy credits each. Paying for arrests was a little unusual, but it was happening more often now that Unidor was essentially the police force of the galaxy.

After the Affiliation of Planets became official a year ago, the organization had been growing by leaps and bounds, and alongside it, Unidor Security. The security company already managed the military operations of the Affiliation, and now more planets were relegating cross-jurisdictional police powers to the company. And because the workload was so great, Unidor farmed out a lot of the work to other security companies, including Starfire Security. Tidus's company was now the second-largest security firm in the galaxy and with new police powers it never had before. Starfire had just moved into a shiny new headquarters building in Dal Innis on the planet Tel'oran. The company had doubled in size in the past year.

Adam was happy for everyone involved, himself included. Which again begged the question: Why was Adam so hellbent on taking jobs with such a high *crazy* quotient? In the brief respites where he thought about the issue, he blamed his cloning. After getting a second lease on life, Adam was bound and determined not to waste it. During his first go around at a lifetime, he more or less let circumstances dictate what happened to him. Now, he wanted to be in more control. And because of that, Adam wanted to experience every thrill in life that was to be had. Sure, he didn't have to swing by a rope from one mile-high-building to the next. He could have figured out another solution, perhaps a different location for the arrest rather than the criminals' most secure local headquarters.

But that wasn't how *The Human* did things. That would have been too simple. Too boring.

Now, his heart raced as he checked his weapons and the backpack he had with him. He had a plan, and it was daring. But first, he had to locate and secure the suspects. Three individuals, each in different locations within a building teeming with guards and then get them all out at the same time. Yeah, fun times for all … unless you asked Charlie.

2

The tracer located the first target three floors above and to the south side of the building. Adam moved to a door in the huge, open-bay room and peeked out into the outside corridor. Charlie could track all flash weapons in the area; in fact, he could trace just about every electronic device in the building since they all used Formilian components. But it was weapons he was most concerned with, although, from the looks of things, just about everyone in the Sylos Syndicate had a damn gun.

It wasn't really called the Sylos Syndicate. Syndicate was just a convenient placeholder translation his language bug provided him. It was something more like *'an affiliation of loyal members coming together for a mutual benefit.'* But that would have been too long to say. But whatever you called them, they were one of the biggest criminal organizations in the galaxy. At least, that was the suspicion. Now, Unidor, with their newfound authority, was ready to move against Sylos to prove that their activities were indeed criminal. Like most conglomerates, a few of their subsidiaries had been found guilty of one thing or another. But, so far, no one had been able to make a charge stick against the upper management. The three 'criminal suspects' Adam was tasked with apprehending could lead to an indictment of the upper crust of Sylos. That was the plan. But first, they had to be arrested.

The only time Adam had arrest authority was when he was the Marshal of Dead Zone back on Navarus. That was fun. He didn't have to wait to be told to apprehend a suspect; he could just do it. And recently, with Starfire, he was chasing fugitives, people who had either jumped bail or escaped from a facility somewhere. Now, Adam was at the front of the line, with authority to take suspects into custody.

Of course, that was an authority that had to be backed up by something. And on the planet Calinan, while ensconced in the belly of the criminal beast, Adam's authority was as ephemeral as a fart in a herd of cows.

And that was why the three suspects were still walking free. No one had found a way to get them away from their power center. So, if the mountain won't come to Mohammed, then Adam would break into Sylos headquarters.

It was Night-1 on Calinan, which was around one a.m.

Human time. As Adam had remarked earlier, he was surprised to find so many active weapons in the building. But this wasn't just a business location. Sylos also maintained a hundred residential suites for their executives at the upper levels. The South Tower was the home of the three suspects, which would make Adam's job a little easier. None had mates or pets that he knew of, and once Adam got inside the suites, he could take his time preparing the suspects for exfiltration.

Adam loved running the planning scenarios through his head. They always sounded so logical, so doable. Reality was the downer in most cases. But so far, Adam Cain had managed to 'luck' or 'skill' out of too many plans to count. This mission, so far, was coming off like clockwork.

To Adam's delight, the hallways had muted lighting appropriate for the late hour, and no one was about. Most of the active weapons Charlie detected were stationary, and those that weren't—carried by the sentries—were easy to monitor. Adam scooted up a stairway for three stories until he came to the floor where the first suspect had his apartment. There were security cameras on every floor and in every hallway, but Charlie had already dealt with that. A negative prompt was added to the recording program that effectively made Adam invisible to the cameras, which was pretty amazing. Adam wondered how he ever got along without an ATD, particularly Charlie's upgraded version. It was as if Adam had a full squad of his SEAL Team Six buddies at his side. He made a note to give Charlie a raise after the mission was over, knowing full well that Charlie worked for free.

Adam came to the door to the suite. Since nearly everything in the galaxy was electronic, it was the same for the lock. And, again, Charlie had that covered. Adam didn't even hesitate before turning the handle and entering the apartment.

Another neat gizmo Adam was employing was a pair of night vision contact lenses, again courtesy of alien technical prowess. They adjusted automatically to the light conditions, making every scene appear mid-day no matter the time. The room was fully lit, with adjustments made for the two hallway lights that still shone.

Adam moved with practiced skill into the main part of the apartment where the living room and kitchen were located. The building had been constructed before Sylos took over most of it, so the plans were a matter of public record. Adam knew the layout of the apartments and where the suspect would be sleeping.

His name was Valos Boz'nickin. He was one of the top accountants for Sylos and would provide valuable insights into the organization's finances if he could be convinced to testify. Adam didn't have much information about how strong a case Unidor had against him that might convince him to turn state's evidence. That wasn't any of The Human's concern. But Unidor knew what they were doing. He would earn his commission and then let the lawyers do their thing.

One of the three bedrooms was to the left, and Adam moved cautiously in that direction. Although he had the layout, he wasn't sure which room Valos would be in. All the bedrooms were suites with balconies, so any of them was as good as the other for the master suite.

The first door he came to was open, and a quick look inside showed it was unoccupied. Adam moved to the next. He slowly opened the door; this room, as well, was unoccupied.

The last door was it. Adam turned the handle, pushed open the door and slipped inside. Sure enough, a single individual occupied the bed. Valos was tall and bulky, filling up most of the huge bed. The mattress was about four feet thick, putting the top of the bed at about five feet. Adam could barely see over the covers to spot his target. The exposed head was V-shaped, which made Adam question where the brain was. Or did he have two brains, one in each section? The thought occupied Adam's mind for only a split second before he moved a small hassock against the bed so he could get a better vantage on the sleeping alien.

And then he leaned over, clamping a hand over the accountant's mouth and a forearm across his neck. Even then, it took a moment for Valos to come fully awake. He didn't react immediately. He had an eye on each section of his split head, and they wandered around lazily until they finally focused on Adam. Then he began to struggle.

The Human was about two feet shorter than the alien but probably weighed as much with his denser bone and muscle structure. Valos bucked under the covers but couldn't get Adam to budge.

"Easy does it, Valos," Adam said while displaying a sly grin. "Yell out, and you die."

The alien was intelligent—he had to be to do the job he did. He obeyed Adam's instructions. Then, expertly, the Human twisted the alien's right arm around, rolling the creature onto his stomach.

The Human pulled a strand of locking straps from his utility belt and fastened it around Velos's wrists. Then he jumped off the bed and motioned for the alien to come to him. The creature was a bean counter, not a soldier, so he complied without question. People like him were valuable, both to the organization he worked for and to law enforcement. He was certain he wouldn't be hurt … if it could be helped.

"Who are you? What do you want?" Velos asked.

Adam continued to grin. "Since you asked—I love doing this part." Adam removed a small card from the front pocket of his shirt and began reading from it. "As a duly-appointed agent of Starfire Security and under agreement with Unidor Security, I hereby place you under arrest. You will be transported to a designated receiving center at which time you will be transferred to the appropriate court for disposition of your case. You may seek professional counsel only after you reach the court of authority. Until that time, you may remain silent. If you choose not to, the arresting officer may relay any and all conversations to the court of authority for use against you. You are further advised not to resist arrest. The arresting officer has the authority to subdue the suspect using whatever force necessary, including lethal. Do you understand these terms?"

Valos nodded.

"Say it aloud," Adam commanded. "I'm recording this."

"I do."

Now, Adam grinned even wider. "I now pronounce us husband and wife."

Valos frowned. "I do not understand."

"Never mind. Just a little arresting officer humor." Adam took his prisoner by the arm. "Now, come with me. You're going to love this. Or maybe not."

Adam led Valos by the arm into the living room before taking off his backpack and pulling out a tangled mess of canvas strapping. "I never know how this thing goes," he said as he untangled the confusing mess. "Turn around."

Velos obeyed.

Adam ran one of the straps under the alien's right arm and then another under his left. Then he snapped the pieces together. Then, he took a longer strap and ran it toward the creature's crotch. "Don't take this wrong, but I need to get a little intimate." Adam threaded a pair of straps between his legs and then up his back, connecting them to the loops around his shoulders.

"What are you doing?" Valos asked.

"Getting you ready for a trip." Adam grimaced. "I'm afraid it won't be very comfortable, but with any luck, you'll survive."

"What are you going to do?"

Adam attached another module to the back of the harness as he casually shrugged toward the patio door. "I'm going to throw you off the balcony," he said matter-of-factly.

Valos reacted badly to the news by opening his mouth to scream and backing away. Adam tugged on one of the front straps, pulling the alien closer. And then he slapped him. It wasn't a hard slap, but for an alien, it was almost enough to knock him out.

"Relax," Adam said. "I've done this myself. It's quite exhilarating, almost like base jumping." The Human shrugged. "Which, I guess, it is, in a way, at least initially. But don't worry. We're high enough that there won't be any real danger."

Next, Adam ran straps around the alien's legs before pulling out a black leather head mask and mouth gag. "Sorry about this, but I don't want you screaming all the way down."

"You … you cannot do this!" Velos pleaded. "I have information, information of value to law enforcement."

"I'm sure you do," Adam acknowledged. "That's why I'm arresting you. But, you see, I have to get you out of the building, and as far as I can see, there's only one way to do that."

Velos protested until he toppled backward onto the plush carpet of his executive-level apartment. Adam straddled him before placing the muffle over his mouth and then the black mask over his head. "Trust me," Adam said. "Having the mask on is a blessing."

With Velos secure on the floor, Adam moved to the patio door and opened it. He stepped out onto the wide and expansive balcony and stepped up to the side. At over four thousand feet in the air, the balcony was higher than any building on Earth that Adam had been in. The wind was strong at this altitude, and the balcony was protected by ten-foot-tall glass panels that blocked the wind but still afforded an incredible view. It was night, but even so, the view was spectacular, looking out at a myriad of other buildings nearly as tall as this one that made up the city of Halmon. But this building complex was the tallest. Adam glanced up, seeing that there were still another hundred floors above him.

From the building plans, Adam knew that the glass barriers surrounding the balcony were hinged halfway up, allowing for the walls to be lowered when the air was calm. He now unhooked a panel and lowered the section until the glass railing was only five feet high.

Adam returned to the living room and dragged Valos

onto the balcony. The alien kicked with his bound legs and screamed through his muffle. Adam ignored him.

"It's best if you don't jerk around too much. The drag chute can get tangled, and if that happens, there are no guarantees. Do you understand?"

Velos shook his head emphatically.

"Oh, well, you'll learn."

Adam leaned the eight-foot-tall alien against the five-foot-high glass panel, bent over and then lifted the alien's legs off the floor and unceremoniously flipped Velos over the side.

The Human looked over the side at the dark figure as it tumbled away. Then, after only a second or two, a small white circle appeared, flopping in the wind. A small delta wing extended farther from the module Adam had placed on the alien's back with guided wings that pulled the falling creature away from the side of the building.

With his night vision contacts, Adam could see what happened next. A black, six-foot-wide drone appeared from along the road separating the massive two-building complex from its neighbors, sweeping in silently and homing in on the drag chute. Forward pinchers on the fuselage opened and lined up on the line between the chute and the falling alien. A moment later, the drone snagged the line, and the pinchers closed.

The UAV was preprogrammed, and now it climbed high, zipping past Adam while towing the bound—and undoubtedly soiled—alien with it. It would take the prisoner to a designated rendezvous point where a sentry bot would keep an eye on him until Adam had all the prisoners in custody.

And so far, the plan was working. One down, two to go.

3

The second capture went pretty much like the first, except this guy was a soldier and didn't take too kindly to being placed under arrest. After knocking him out, Adam recorded him reading his alien Miranda Rights to him before repeating the process, dumping him over the side with much less fanfare than with Valos. Adam thought maybe that was the way to do it. Dispense with the pleasantries and just knock them unconscious before tossing them off the building. In the long run, they would probably appreciate him doing that. The roving drone scooped up the next alien and transferred him to Adam's makeshift holding cell.

The last target was named Daxian Pannel, and he lived on the highest floor, meaning he was the biggest of the bigwigs. He also had live security outside his room. Charlie tracked the active flash weapons and disarmed them while giving Adam their exact locations. The Human had MK flash weapons, along with his trusty hybrid kinetic/energy weapon. He used neither on the guards. Instead, he had instant-acting tranquilizer darts, which he expertly placed into their necks in about a half-second flat. However, when one of the guards fell, his utility belt caught the side of a table in the hallway and tipped it over. The corridor was carpeted, but it still caused more noise than Adam was comfortable with.

The Human moved up to the door, the dart gun still in his hand. Daxian was a big mother, and Adam wasn't taking any chances that a stun bolt could put him down and a higher setting on the weapon might kill him. Each one of these arrests was worth two-hundred-fifty thousand ECs; he didn't want to risk his commission by being stupid.

All clear, Charlie reported. *I detect no electronic movement in the apartment. No lights have come on.*

Thank you, Adam thought.

Adam opened the door and stepped across the threshold. His day-light vision spotted someone cutting across the corridor about twenty feet away. He rushed forward, knowing that Daxian knew he was there.

Just then, another figure appeared out of the corner of Adam's right eye. It came like a blur and from a side room. A shiny metal pole crashed down on his head, sending Adam to the floor, his vision fuzzy and his senses dulled. His incapacity only lasted a second, but it was long enough for the massive figure to step forward and plant a solid foot into the Human's stomach. The force of the blow lifted Adam off the floor and into the wall. When he fell back down, Daxian hit him again with the metal rod, this time across the back. Much of that blow was absorbed by the backpack and harness Adam wore, but it still hurt. This was no ordinary alien he was fighting and if he didn't do something quick, it may be too late.

But then Daxian jumped on his back and brought the metal rod across the front of Adam's body, lifting it until it pressed against his throat. Then powerful arms began to pull, choking the Human. Adam fought with all his strength to keep the pipe from crushing his trachea while pushing off with his legs and lifting the two fighters into the air. Then Adam jerked backward, sending them both to the floor with Daxian on his back and Adam on top of him, still fighting to keep the rod from strangling him.

Just then, a manic-looking naked alien female rushed at Adam from within the apartment. She bounced and landed on him, clawing his face, hands and arms like a wild animal. While fending off the blows from the female, Adam managed to get an arm pressed up from his shoulder and between his body and the metal rod. He screamed in pain as his right shoulder dislocated again, allowing him to slip in. The pain subsided, and with the threat of being strangled momentarily gone, Adam was able to free his left hand. He sent a short jab into the chin of the crazy naked alien, which was enough to knock her out. The limp body slipped off of him.

Adam now sent his left elbow into Daxian's ribs. The hit was clean and powerful and made an impact. The beast roared with pain into Adam's left ear. The grip lessened slightly on the rod, and that's when Adam threw back his head, smashing his skull into the alien's nose.

That was enough for Daxian to abandon his grip on Adam and push him away. The Human staggered to his feet, choking and holding his throat as Daxian leisurely stood up, the metal rod still in his hand. He growled menacingly, twirling the five-foot-long rod in his hand with expert precision.

Adam reached for his MK, only to have his right arm fail to respond. His shoulder was dislocated again, rendering his arm useless. He stepped back, barely out of reach of the swinging rod and reached across his body with his left hand for his weapon. The movement was awkward, and as Adam pulled the weapon from its holster, it came out backward. And as if that wasn't enough, Daxian slapped the weapon away with the metal rod.

Adam now backtracked, moving into the living area almost at a backward run. He went to duck a full-on swing of the rod but fell over a coffee table instead. It probably saved his life. But Daxian wasn't done. He continued with his swing, spinning in place and then bringing the rod down on the shattered glass table. Adam barely had time to roll away.

As he stood, Daxian charged in, dropping a broad shoulder into the much smaller Human. Adam was sent flying through the air and through the glass patio door onto the balcony. The glass in the doors and windows at this height was designed to withstand hurricane-force winds, so it took a lot of force to break them. Adam's battered body did the job effortlessly.

Adam was barely conscious at this point, crawling on his hands and knees to get away from the lumbering giant. Then he felt boulder-size hands grip his harness, and a moment later, Adam Cain was soaring through the air, having been tossed off the side of the two-hundred-ninety-eighth floor of the South Tower.

Daxian Pannel walked with satisfaction up to the glass railing of the balcony. It was only five feet high since, at the moment, this side of the building was shielded from most of the high winds. He glanced over the side at the darkness below, snorting once before turning to return to the living room. He had just passed over the threshold of the shattered patio door, being careful not to step on any of the broken glass with his bare feet, when a horrendous crash sounded behind him. He turned just in time to see the small pink creature come blasting through a panel of glass railing and fly into Daxian, sending the two bodies tumbling into the living room. The small creature was on top of him, pummeling him with powerful blows, more powerful than he's ever been hit with before. Daxian was stunned but managed to gain enough awareness to notice a long, heavy strap trailing out from the back of his attacker's harness and ending in a dainty-looking miniature parachute that fluttered in the wind on the balcony.

Daxian gripped the strap and attempted to wrap it around the neck of the smaller beast. And *beast* was the only description he could come up with. This thing, although small, was ferocious and incredibly strong. Where once he thought he could get the best of this creature, now he had his doubts.

Daxian managed to roll to his right and stagger to his feet. The tiny beast wasn't much better off than he was, and for a moment, the two of them stood panting in their blood and sweat. But then anger got the best of Daxian. He was much larger than the pink beast with the yellow hair atop his head. He would let his mass do the fighting.

He rushed forward, tackling the smaller creature and lifting him off the ground. But then Daxian's bare foot stepped on a large piece of glass, splitting it open. He cried out in pain and released the beast. Then he turned and staggered through the broken doorway, stepping on more glass. He stumbled and lost his balance. With arms flailing, Daxian Pannel tumbled through the broken glass railing and into the great void of darkness beyond the building.

. . .

"Oh crap!" Adam yelled. He gripped the strap for the drogue chute and ran for the balcony, diving headfirst over the side. His day/night vision allowed him to spot the falling alien immediately. He sighted his target and tucked his arms and legs to his side, becoming an arrow falling through the night sky.

Adam and Daxian collided, but rather than reach out to Adam for dear life, the alien began swiping at him, his eyes fierce and insane. The Human did his best to dodge the hits, but tumbling through the air almost five thousand feet in the air didn't give him anywhere to hide. Then Daxian reached for the chute strap again, taking the flailing length and trying to get it wrapped around Adam's neck.

"Stop it, you maniac!" Adam yelled over the roar of the wind in his ears. "I'm trying to save you."

But Daxian wouldn't listen.

Just then, the pair rolled again, and the drogue strap wrapped around their bodies, with a length of it now wrapping around Daxian's neck. Adam clawed at the cord, but the alien was fighting him.

Then, off to his left, Adam saw the drone angling in for a catch. There were twenty feet of strap trailing out above Adam with the tiny white parachute on the end. It would be a simple catch.

But Daxian's neck was still wrapped in the strapping.

Then it was too late. The pinchers on the drone gripped the strap and closed before the craft angled up sharply, stopping Adam's fall. The cord tightened instantly around the alien's neck, ripping it savagely off his shoulders. Adam was sprayed with blood as he watched the severed head and torso grow smaller by the second, falling to the ground now only fifteen hundred feet below.

Adam continued to look down as the drone automatically followed its original programming and flew off high above the Twin Towers. Only a minute later, it landed five miles from the buildings at the far end of a dark forested park next to a bulky alien cargo van. Adam's two previous 'suspects' were on the ground with the big soldier still unconscious, while Valos, the accountant, lay whimpering with his black mask still on and smelling like the shit he'd expelled as he fell through the night sky before being snagged by the drone. The sentry bot sat obediently off to one side, a stun rod in its hand, with nothing to do.

Adam climbed unsteadily to his feet off the cool grass of the park and unhooked the drogue line from his harness. He glanced over at the imposing edifice of the Twin Towers, which seemed to climb all the way into space from this vantage point. He blew out his breath.

"Damn, that was a rush."

I am glad you think so, said Charlie in his mind. *Now, there is an increased police presence in the area as your handiwork is being reported. I would suggest we get moving.*

"I don't know, Charlie," Adam said as he opened the back of the van and dragged his two prisoners into the back. "You're becoming a real nag."

Someone has to keep you focused.

Adam grinned—painfully. He must really be hurt to feel the pain as acutely as he did. His right shoulder and arm were virtually useless, and his ribs and back felt as if they were on fire. He would have six days to mend on the way to the receiving station, where he'd turn over his prisoners. After that, another week to Tel'oran. That should just about do it.

The sentry bot climbed in the back of the van while the drone lifted off and settled on top of the van, using magnetic clamps to lock it in place. Then, Adam climbed into the driver's compartment and lowered the windows. Valos's stink was overpowering, and Adam still had a twenty-minute drive to the spaceport.

He would get his prisoners secured and Valos a new set of clothes before tossing his old set of sleeping garments out the airlock.

As Adam drove, he glanced back at this cargo. Two—not three—prisoners. But then he remembered a song from his childhood by one of his favorite singers, and he grinned.

"Don't feel bad, 'cause two out of three ain't bad," he sang, with only the creatures of the night on this alien world to critique him. He didn't think he sounded half bad.

He was sure Tidus wouldn't see it that way.

4

Adam landed the *Arieel* at the executive spaceport and had it moved to his space. After hooking up to shore power and sewer, he took his personal transport into downtown Dal Innis and the just-completed Starfire Security Building.

The damn thing was ninety stories tall and gleamed in the morning light. The workday on this part of Tel'oran was well underway, and Adam was happy to see all the people coming and going to the new building. Because of alien technology, the structure only took eight months to construct from idea to grand opening. It had been operating for four months, two of which Adam had been off the planet. He had a private office somewhere in the edifice if he could remember where.

With the rapid growth of Starfire recently, the company occupied most of the building, although some of the lower floors were rented out to smaller businesses. Adam smiled, thinking about the humble beginnings when he and Tidus first mentioned starting their own company. Unfortunately, at the time, Adam wasn't ready to commit to a management position. He had been recently cloned and had a whole new life to live. He wasn't ready to be tied to a desk. Instead, Tidus agreed to a lucrative compensation package—better than anyone else in the company—and the legend of *The Human* was born. Although Adam's pay was less stable than Tidus's, he still made a king's fortune. That's king with a small 'K.' Now, he had enough in savings to cushion some of the ups and downs of security work, of missions gone bust or collateral damage he couldn't avoid reimbursing.

Again, Adam questioned some of his more recent decisions regarding missions and tactics. There was definitely something going on in the back of his mind, and sooner or later, he'd have to face it head-on. Where was he going in life, and what did he want out of it? And the ultimate question of all: What would it take to make him happy?

At the moment, he couldn't honestly say.

Tidus wanted to see Adam as soon as he returned to the planet; he always wanted to see the Human the moment he arrived, either to congratulate him or to chew him out. The fact that Adam had lost a third of the fee for the arrest of the three suspects, Adam could see the conversation going either way. He'd already sent a mission debrief to the Juirean, so Tidus knew how hard it had been making the arrests. It was a miracle Adam was able to pull it off in the first place. But then, again, this was Tidus Fe Nolan we were speaking about, the original, green-skinned *Scrooge of the Milky Way.*

Adam made his way up to executive row on the eighty-fifth floor, where all the top executives had their offices, Adam included. The other ten floors above were reserved for a pair of fancy restaurants open to the public, plus one for the executives exclusively. Hey, rank had its privileges, and Adam was okay with that. The four employee breakrooms were pretty damn nice in their own right. With so much money flowing into Starfire these days, Tidus and his architects spared no expense in making the revamped Starfire the envy of the industry.

Tidus was in the hallway when Adam exited the elevator, surprising him.

"Good timing," Tidus said. "Follow me."

Adam furrowed his brow and followed.

The Juirean led him down the corridor in the opposite direction from Tidus's office before he opened a lacquered paneled door and entered a room at the opposite side of the building. It was almost as large as Tidus's office. Strangely, Tidus moved around the desk and sat down.

That was when Adam noticed all of the Juirean's personal belongings and mementos were in the room.

"Have a seat," Tidus motioned with his hand.

The office had a spectacular view of the city, looking north toward the mountains. Adam couldn't decide whether it was better here or in his other—old?—office.

"You moved?" Adam asked as he sank down into an obscenely comfortable chair in front of the large stone desk. Juireans were known for their stone desks, and this one, Adam knew, had come all the way from Juir, having been salvaged from the remains of the Malor Building and rumored to have been used by Oplim Ra Unic himself, one of the founders of Juirean society. The provenance of the desk was impossible to verify, but it made for a good story.

"I *have* moved," Tidus confirmed. "But we will speak on that later. Now, about the mission."

Adam grimaced. So, it was going to be a scolding.

"That was quite the show you put on, flying through the air like *Dazalim*."

"Who's *Dazalim*?"

Tidus waved an impatient hand. "Not important, just a fantasy character from Juirean lure. Now, I know this change in mission character is a little hard for you to grasp, but we cannot go around killing arrest suspects."

"I know that," Adam snapped. "But I tried to save him. He's the one that wouldn't cooperate. It's all in the report."

"I know; I read it. And I agree, you tried. But after all the effort it took to get in the building, perhaps you should have just stunned him and kept him under for the bulk of the mission."

Adam frowned. "That was the plan. But now, you're second-guessing my missions?"

"I've always second-guessed your missions. It's just that in this case, you may have screwed up—unintentionally," Tidus said quickly.

"Why, what's happened?"

"It seems the guy that died—Daxian Pannel—is the brother of the head of the Sylos Syndicate."

"The criminal cartel?" said Adam with mock surprise. "Of course; I knew that going in. But I didn't know that about Daxian."

Tidus wrinkled his face into a grimace. Juirean grimaces were hideous expressions. "Most of the law enforcement agencies don't call them a cartel. They're beyond that. If there is ever an example of Human organized crime in the galaxy, it would be Sylos. No one knows how big they are, with some saying they would come in third behind Xan-fi and Maris-Kliss, not counting their affiliated sponsors."

"Such as Galena Gar," Adam said, a fond memory slipping through his mind.

"Yeah, I know," Tidus smirked. "You and Galena had a *moment* together, once, for a few seconds, in the back of a transport. I don't think that warrants that dreamy look on your face."

Adam grinned, bouncing his eyebrows. "Who knows, Tidus? There's a saying on Earth: *que sera, sera*. Whatever will be, will be."

"Well, keep dreaming, Mr. Cain. I know you think you have these magical pheromones that make Humans irresistible—"

"Hey, that's the way the Aris made us. It's documented!"

Tidus shook his head. "That doesn't mean every female in the galaxy will melt in your presence."

Adam shrugged.

"Now, back to serious matters," Tidus said. "Apparently, Davos Pannel is a little upset that his baby brother was killed. So, just as you may have seduced Galena Gar, you could have just as easily made an enemy out of another powerful citizen of the galaxy and one who's a lot more ruthless."

"Daxian died; he wasn't killed," Adam corrected.

"Tell that to Davos—on second thought, don't. I think you should lay low for a while. Let things settle out. The other two you arrested could provide testimony that could distract Davos from any thoughts of revenge. Let's let that run its course."

Adam looked around the new office. "So, you're not mad at me, not going to dock my pay?"

Tidus smiled. "I never said that. In fact, I have some

announcements to make, a few changes I've implemented since you've been gone."

"Like a new office? What was wrong with the old one?"

"Nothing," Tidus answered. "It's just that it would be a little crowded in there, seeing that someone else now has the space."

"Who?" Adam asked, genuinely curious. Tidus's office had been designed as the showcase for the entire company, as much a place to impress as it was to work in. It had been featured in broadcasts on Tel'oran as the latest and best example of corporate opulence.

Adam waited patiently. Whatever musical desks were being played at headquarters didn't affect him.

"I've relinquished day-to-day operations of the company to what on Earth would be called a Chief Executive Officer. It's someone you know well … Vinset."

Adam's jaw fell open. "*Vinset!* You put Vinset in charge?"

The intensity of his comment may have given Tidus the wrong impression, so Adam spoke quickly to clarify any misunderstandings.

"Don't get me wrong, I think that's great!" he said. "Not that you've stepped down, but that Vinset is very capable. I think it's a great choice. But … but why?"

Tidus leaned back in his chair and looked out the expansive window at the snowy mountains. There was a whisp of clouds hugging the peaks, making the scene picture-perfect.

"With the growth the company has experienced recently, running the entire show has become quite a burden. And you know me; I'm a hands-on manager. But now we're diversifying, going into more traditional police work rather than mainly hunting fugitives. The job was taking all my time as it was. It's to the point where I can't handle it all by myself anymore. Vinset is mature, serious and highly intelligent. And he has the energy to do the job. I'll still be his boss and have the final say, but I'll let Vinset handle the details while I look at the bigger picture. Besides, not all of us can get a second lifetime handed to us—like some people we know. I'm not getting any younger, and I have other interests I wish to pursue."

Adam grinned. "You do? I thought you lived and breathed Starfire."

"I still do," Tidus said. "But now, something else has caught my attention."

"A woman—a female, excuse me?" Adam gasped. "You old devil you!"

"No, it is nothing like that." Tidus stretched out an impossibly wide grin of his own. "You are looking at the newest candidate for the Planetary Council on Tel'oran. That's right, I'm going into politics!"

The smile vanished from Adam's face. "Politics? Why the hell would you do that? Talk about rubbing elbows was the slimiest creatures on the planet."

"And that is why I want to do this. I have been on Tel'oran for a long time now, and I have built a very good reputation. A group approached me and asked if I would be interested. They think having a Juirean on the Council would be impressive for their side." Then his face turned serious. "And after seeing how far Nasin would go to achieve the Eldership of the Authority, it got me thinking of what good I could do."

Adam nodded. It had been a little over a year since Tidus watched his brother walk off the side of the Kacoran Plain on Juir. After that, Tidus wasn't the same. He didn't joke as much, and he remained locked in his office—the one in the old Starfire building while the new one was being built. But once the new headquarters was completed, he seemed to come out of his shell, becoming more of the Tidus of old. Still, it had changed him inside. To what degree, Adam was just now coming to realize.

"If that's what you want, then go for it," the Human said. "And maybe someday, you'll be the president of Tel'oran, maybe even move to be part of the leadership council for the Affiliation. The sky's the limit, my old friend."

Adam was truly happy for Tidus; at least he knew what would make him happy.

Adam gripped the arms of the chair and prepared to stand up. "Can I assume my office is still in the same place, or did I get moved, too?"

"Hold on a minute, Adam. There's more to tell you."

Adam pursed his lips and sank back into the cushions.

Tidus took a datapad from a drawer in his desk and handed it to Adam.

"It's all done; everything is official and recorded," Tidus said before Adam could even begin to read the legal documents on the screen.

"What is this?" he asked.

"These are transfer documents and recordings giving you, Adam Cain, twenty-five percent ownership of Starfire Security."

Adam shook his head and laid the datapad back on the desk. "Thanks, but no thanks, Tidus. I'm not ready to occupy the office next to Vinset, dealing with employee complaints and work orders all day."

Tidus smiled. "It's nothing like that. And besides, it's done. You have no choice in it."

"What do you mean I have no choice? I can say no."

"But why would you? These documents give you ownership, along with all the benefits that entails. They do not, however, assign you any responsibility, only that which you wish to take. You are like a shareholder, only more. Adam, this is a windfall! Starfire is worth several billion energy credits, and now you get twenty-five percent of all the profits. Vinset and I still run the company, although you could step in at any time and make decisions. You even have authority over Vinset. The only person higher in the company is me."

Adam was stunned. "What? Why are you doing this? Does it have anything to do with Nasin?"

Tidus's face turned dark. "In truth, it does, but not in the way you imagine. What you did—for me, for the galaxy—was above and beyond. I know you had a financial incentive to take care of him, or at least you thought you did. But it got me thinking about all the times you have helped me and the company. Starfire is only in the position we're in now because you saved the planet Tactori from my deranged brother. You saved the Affiliation, and you saved Unidor. And that's just part of a long list of 'saves' you've made in your double lifetime, going so far as to save the galaxy at least three times that I know of. None of us would be here if not for you. And now, I see you still taking inordinate risks on silly missions, and I wonder why?"

Adam smirked. "You're not the only one," he said softly.

"Well, with this, you can pick and choose what missions you want to take and those you don't. You won't have to do anything for the credits any longer. Adam, you, more than anyone in the galaxy, deserve a reward. And now you're into your second life, and you're still working for a living. That may be what makes you happy, but now, you have a choice. Seek the thrills however you want, but just know it will be *your* choice and not to appease anyone else."

Adam was stunned, absolutely stunned. A myriad of

thoughts were bouncing around in his head, not the least of which was the fact that Adam Cain was now fabulously wealthy. He had no idea how wealthy he was since he never paid that much attention to the profitability of Starfire, only his own profitability. But he'd watched the growth of Starfire over the past few years. It was something to behold.

And now Tidus wanted to go into politics. And Vinset was running Starfire.

Damn, Adam had only been gone from Tel'oran for thirty-eight days. A lot had changed in that time.

And now Adam was swept up in that whirlwind of change. He had no idea how this would change him, his life or his way of living.

"Adam, snap out of it!" Tidus said, snapping his fingers. "I know this is overwhelming. But don't wig out on me now."

Adam always liked the way Tidus spoke more like a Human than most Humans he knew, of which there were very few and none on Tel'oran. Suddenly, an incredible wave of nostalgia swept over him. He knew what caused it. He had just been given some incredible, life-altering news ... and he had no one to share it with and certainly no one who knew what it meant to him. The only people who could even vaguely relate were now in their mid-to-high seventies and living on Earth: Sherri Valentine and Riyad Tarazi. They were getting older but still going strong. Seeing that Adam suddenly had a lot more free time, a trip to Earth was called for. And—for what it was worth—it might be time to share the wealth with some of his old friends. Adam could never have done all the things he'd done without them. Along with Copernicus Smith, Summer Rains, and Kaylor and Jym. But especially Tidus.

Adam's eyes were sopping wet when he looked at the big green alien. His eyes were also moist, making Adam think that he'd never seen a Juirean cry before. He never knew they could. But everything cries ... doesn't it?

When Adam staggered out of Tidus's office a few minutes later, he wasn't too shocked to find Vinset and Siri in the lobby outside, big grins on both their faces.

"You knew?" he said to his friends.

"Consider, Adam," Vinset said, frowning, "I am now the head of Starfire Security; of course I knew. I had to sign off on the statements before they became final. Not really," Vinset laughed. "But it does make me sound important. In reality, I now work for you. What is your bidding, my master?"

"How about hugs all around?"

And Adam got his wish. But then he stepped back from Siri, looking down at her slightly protruding belly on her lithe, feline body.

"What ... what is this?" he asked, concern in his tone.

Siri and Vinset beamed back at him. They had been a couple for a few years now, but this was ... different.

They were of two different species, and the only interspecies mating that produced a child that Adam knew of was his and Arieel's daughter, Lila. Of course, that had been the intention of the ancient Aris when they started their Grand Experiment to produce the Apex Being three billion years ago. They succeeded when Lila turned out to be an immortal mutant genius with incredible powers. Would Siri and Vinset's child turn out the same? After all, Siri was a mutant in her own right.

"Relax, Adam," Siri said. She and Vinset knew the story of Lila. "There is nothing special about my pregnancy. We used a service on my planet to impregnate me. The girl will be of my species, but Vinset and I will raise her as our own."

More tears now flowed from Adam's already red and moist eyes, which only started the flow in Siri and Vinset. Again, more hugs.

"This is what I get for leaving town for a month," Adam said, choking up. "Next time, I won't stay away so long."

"You promise?" Siri said, hugging him again.

He felt a sweet tingle in his mind. Siri was a true telepath who could not only read minds but also alter emotions. Adam's ATD kept him from being probed by her, but he still felt her presence. It was just a little mental hug to go along with the physical.

After that, the three of them met Tidus in the executive restaurant on the ninety-fourth floor for a celebratory lunch. And there was a lot to celebrate. A lot to be thankful for.

Adam was walking on air when he left the Starfire Building three hours later. He was in a mild state of shock at the sudden turn his life had taken. He stopped and turned to look at the gleaming and glistening structure. Maybe he would find the happiness he longed for by spending a little more time here.

Even though they weren't Human, Adam had friends in that building, real friends. Perhaps that was what he was missing. Adam can save the galaxy many times over, but unless he had someone to share his victories with—along with his failures—the actions seemed hollow. Even now, he would return to the *Arieel* and share the good news with … with whom? Charlie? His ATD's AI already knew. And Beth would accept his boasting but simply as new data input, with the possibility of a little artificial emotion thrown in. And even if he called Sherri and Riyad on Earth, they would be happy for him, up to the time the link broke and they went back to their real lives.

Damn, was Adam Cain … lonely? If so, then the cure for his melancholy was inside the steel and glass edifice facing him. The beautiful, gleaming structure … that now exploded in his face.

. . .

The concussion threw him across the street and through a frontage window. Through his mind's eye, Adam saw a wall of concrete come crashing down on him while a choking cloud of dust and debris blasted through the downtown district of Dal Innis. The sound was so horrific that it knocked out his hearing to the point where only muddled roars and screams could be heard. Through all this tumult, Adam felt his cloning juice soar to new strength in his body. But even that wasn't enough to prevent the coming doom. As Adam Cain quickly faded into unconsciousness, he was sure he would never wake up again. And there were no immortal mutant geniuses around this time to save him.

5

His hearing came back first, the steady, metronome-like bleeping of a heart monitor. Then, the antiseptic smell of a medical facility, probably a hospital, from the otherwise tranquil sensation he received. As his eyes fluttered open, Adam found himself in a hospital bed with metal rails raised on the sides and tubes with liquid in them leading to and from his body. He painfully twisted his head to either side, finding he was alone.

Instantly, memory returned, and unlike when the memories were first etched in his mind, he was able to slow them down and analyze the images that flashed by.

Twin fiery blasts had shot out from the Starfire Building as he stood looking at it from perhaps a hundred feet away. Then, the blurred image of him flying through the air before his senses dulled. And then, with his limp body acting like a thrown rag doll, he crashed against objects but with no feelings, no sensation. His mind continued to register images, but they made little sense. He was buried, and the lights went out, along with his awareness.

And then he woke up in the hospital bed. His pulse raced as a tingle crawled down his spine. He was in a hospital room … and he was alone.

There was no one there watching and waiting for him to recover. No Tidus, no Siri, no Vinset.

And why would they be here? They were in the building when it exploded. Where Adam was thrown clear of the crumbling structure, how could they have possibly survived? What miracle of fate would have spared them?

Adam inhaled sharply as tears drained from his eyes. His last thoughts were still strong in his consciousness, the thoughts of … of the love he felt for the trio of aliens. The awareness of his feelings had only just surfaced when suddenly they were stripped away. What cruel and sick twist of fate would do that to him? He didn't deserve it.

Just then, his dismay was interrupted when a native Tel'oran nurse entered the room. She wasn't shocked to find him awake, but her face was confused.

"Please, remain calm," she said professionally. "I have summoned the doctor. He will be here momentarily. We were not expecting you to awaken so soon." Then she scanned the monitors. "And to recover so quickly. Honestly, I am at a loss…"

"The others?" Adam asked through a larynx that hadn't been used in a while. Even with his elevated tolerance to pain, he still felt the burning in his throat.

"I have no information on the others you inquire of. This facility, along with several others, has been deluged with victims from the catastrophe. In time, you can check the roster." Then she shrugged. "For a while, we thought you would be on the list of casualties and not the recovering. But apparently, miracles do happen."

Adam knew it was no miracle, at least not in the usual sense of the word. His continual cloning helped him survive, as well as recover enough to be aware of his surroundings. It was a good bet no one who was injured as badly would recover this fast if they'd recover at all.

The native doctor came in with an entourage of assistants. He seemed as perplexed over Adam's state of recovery as the nurse. But rather than be happy for Adam's condition, the doctor seemed angry. He was mad at himself because he couldn't explain it.

And then the questioning began, along with a bevy of tests. This confounded the medical experts even more, as each time a test was run, Adam recovered a little bit more, making the prior results obsolete. Finally, the doctor gave up.

"I was assigned your case because I have experience treating Humans," he said by way of explanation. "But even then, I cannot explain what I am witnessing. Do *you* have an explanation?"

"I do," Adam said. His voice was stronger now, as was the rest of his body. What wasn't getting better was his patience. Even after two days of around-the-clock treatment and tests, no one had answered his questions about his comrades from Starfire. "I was part of a medical program on Earth that enhanced my body's ability to tolerate pain and heal faster," Adam lied. Even as fantastical as this story went, it was more believable than the reality that he'd died once and been brought back to life by a pair of mutants who then set about cloning him. The doctor seemed satisfied with a secret medical experiment by the military of Earth. He would accept that explanation for now.

"So, how *do* you feel?" the alien asked.

"I feel good enough to stand," Adam barked. "Now, I want to find out what happened to my friends in the Starfire Building."

The doctor produced a datapad from a deep pocket in his medical robe. He turned it on and scanned the screens. "It has been two weeks since the explosion. Although recovery teams are still sifting through the debris, the preliminary reports show two hundred-eight dead. The casualty count would have been substantially higher, but the explosives were set to the south side of the building, so only about half of the structure collapsed. Even so, there are forty-eight individuals still here or in various hospitals in the area. At this facility, we have the bulk of them, twenty-one."

"Do you have the names?"

"I do, but I cannot reveal them."

"Why not!"

"Privacy issues. Only relatives have been notified."

Adam went to get off the bed. A pair of orderlies came and attempted to hold him down.

"You may think you are well enough to walk, but you are not," the doctor explained. Then he shook his head. "However, at the rapid rate of your recovery, I could allow you out of bed for a few hours beginning tomorrow. Please relax, Adam Cain. Give your body another twelve hours. I beg of you."

So, they knew his name. Only the deep files within Starfire knew his true identity. Otherwise, he was listed on pay and employment records as simply *The Human*. Adam always thought that was a system destined for doom. What would happen if Starfire ever hired another Human? Then Adam would become *The Human #1*. An awkward way of addressing someone…

Adam gave the doctor half a day, but by Night-1—one pm—he was up and staggering weakly through the quiet corridors of the hospital. He'd learned that most of the patients from the bombing were housed in this wing and the one next to it. Each room he passed had a name slipped into a pouch on the door, and he checked them as he walked along. He recognized some of the names but not even half of them. Since Starfire's rapid growth over the past year, the company has been hiring hundreds of new agents and support staff. Even so, there were far too few names he recognized to make him confident.

And then he found Siri.

He opened the door and slipped inside, his heart pounding with anticipation. A soft nightlight lit the room, and evening lights shone through the large window set against the outer wall. Siri was propped up on the bed, asleep, with one arm in an overhead traction harness and a brace on her left leg. Half of her face was covered in a gauze bandage.

Her delicate whiskers flickered, and her nose twitched as her senses told her someone was in the room. Adam didn't have to wake her. Golden, cat-like eyes shot open, instinct taking over.

"Adam!" she cried out, both vocally and in his head. Even with his ATD protecting access to his mind, the impact was forceful.

Adam leaned over and carefully hugged her as tears flooded from both their eyes. There was hardly a place he could touch where she wasn't bandaged or braced.

"Oh, Adam, it was horrible," Siri said between sobs. "Besides Vinset, you're the only one from the building I have seen."

"The same here. I've been checking the door labels. What about Tidus?"

And then Adam looked down at the alien's slender form under the sheet and blanket.

Siri gagged as more tears flowed down her narrow cheeks. "I am no longer pregnant. From what I was told, it was a choice: me or the baby. Since I was not conscious at the time, they chose me. That is not the choice I would have made."

Adam gripped her slender hand and squeezed gently. "I'm so sorry. Does Vinset know—"

The moment he asked the question, he regretted it. Siri broke down again. Adam let her lean over onto his chest, sobbing for several minutes before she regained her composure.

"Being mated, we were in the same room for a while … until he expired. He never regained consciousness to know about me or the baby. In a way, he was spared even more pain."

"And Tidus?"

"From what I have been told, he survived, although he is in a coma."

"Is he here, in this hospital?" Adam asked.

"He is, although I know not where. Adam, it was horrific," Siri repeated. "How did you survive?"

"I was already outside when the bomb went off."

Siri's face hardened. "Yes, it was a bomb; it was intentional! And from what I have been told, they targeted the south side of the building, the side where Vinset had his office. I was on a lower floor on the north side at the time. That is the only reason I survived."

Adam frowned, a question crossing his mind. "How long did Vinset have the office—Tidus's old office?"

"Only a few days." Siri's eyes widened, grasping the meaning of Adam's question. "They targeted Tidus! Or at least the leadership of Starfire!"

Adam nodded. "It makes sense. And Tidus's office, from what I've seen, was pretty well known, having been featured in a number of local broadcasts."

"Who did this, Adam?" Siri asked anger now painted on her fierce, feline features.

Adam snorted, shaking his head. "Where do I begin? We tend to piss off a lot of people just doing our job." Then Adam's face hardened. "But one thing is clear: I *will* find out who did this, and when I do, well, I think you can guess the rest."

Siri pushed herself up more in the bed. "And when you do, I will be—" She winced with pain before falling back on the pillows.

"You just take care of yourself first. I've got this." Adam stood up. "Now, you rest. I'm going to look for Tidus."

"Come back whenever you like. It is only the two of us now. I need your strength."

Adam nodded and then stepped out into the hall. He fell against the wall, his breath coming in fits as the brave façade faded. Vinset was dead … and Tidus was in a coma still two weeks later. Starfire Security was in ruins, and this barely scratched the surface of the tragedy. How could things have turned so bad so fast? Adam was having trouble holding it together, not that he was going to collapse into a pool of self-pity, but because he wanted to kill something, break something, rip someone's spine out. Unfortunately, the list was too long for him to put a face to this horror, at least not yet. But what he told Siri was true. He would find out who did this, and he would make them pay.

Fifteen minutes later, Adam found Tidus's room. When he entered, a pair of nurses were tending to him. They protested his presence at first until they recognized him. Most of the staff on the floor knew of the Human who had healed miraculously fast. And besides that, they saw the concern and determination on Adam's face. He didn't have to ask how Tidus was doing; the natives volunteered the information.

"Your friend has severe swelling of the brain. We have ventilated and are draining fluid every six hours. It continues to build up. In addition, he has a collapsed lung and a broken left leg."

"From what we were told, his office was on the ninetieth floor," said the other nurse. "When half of the building collapsed, his office was exposed. The section of floor he was on was barely intact. Rescuers got to him only minutes before the floor crumbled."

"The prognosis?" Adam mumbled.

Mirrored expressions said it all.

"Tell me, please," Adam pleaded.

The lead nurse stepped up to him. "It does not look promising. He has been like this since he was brought in. And even if by some miracle he survives, there will be no telling what mental capacities he retains."

"I need to talk to his doctor," Adam announced emphatically. "There may be something I can do."

"Are you a doctor?"

"No," Adam answered. "Just get him for me if you can, please. I need to speak with him as soon as possible."

"It is night; he is not in the hospital," said the head nurse. "However, he will be here in the morning. Please return to your room. I will have him call on you in the morning."

"Thank you," Adam said sincerely. Then, with one last clenched-jaw look at Tidus, Adam left and returned to his room.

The next morning, Adam was feeling even stronger, nearly completely healed from his injuries. His doctor now stood in the hallway, speaking in hushed tones with Tidus's doctor. After a few moments, they both entered the room.

"I am Simfas Vicanon," announced the alien doctor.

He wasn't Tel'oran, but from the way he carried himself, Adam got the impression he was a bigwig at the hospital. The powers that be had to know who Tidus was; he was pretty well-known across Tel'oran. He would command the very best care available.

"I understand you wish to speak to me."

Adam looked at the pair of nurses doing their chores and frowned. Simfas got the message and asked them to step outside for a moment. When it was only Adam and the two doctors, Adam waved them closer.

"I wasn't completely honest with you, Doctor Klastor," he began, addressing his doctor. "But now I'm going to tell you a story that must not leave this room. If it does, I will take that as a personal affront and seek revenge, which is the best way I can say it. Do you understand?"

Although both medical professionals appeared insulted by Adam's tone, they nodded. Even to those not in the security business, nearly everyone on Tel'oran knew of *The Human*. And the doctors now knew he had a name: Adam Cain. What they didn't know—not yet—was that he was *that* Adam Cain.

"I don't know if this will help, but within my body, I have a process taking place that allows me to heal exceptionally fast and to virtually ignore pain."

Dr. Klastor nodded. "As I told you," he said to Simfas. "Although I have had some experience treating Humans, there were readings present that I could not begin to understand." He looked at Adam. "You told me yesterday of the secret experiments done on you. We would sincerely wish to learn of these procedures."

Adam snorted. "As I said, I wasn't completely honest. I wasn't part of a secret experiment. It's much more than that?"

"Does it have anything to do with the object under your skin beneath your right armpit?" Klastor asked.

Adam laughed. "Believe it or not, it doesn't. That's something else. Now…" Adam leaned back in the bed as the doctors took seats. "Let me tell you the truth. It will be hard to accept, but every word is true." He grinned slightly. "I assume the two of you have heard of the mutants Panur and Lila." The physicians nodded, frowns on their faces. "Well, my story begins on the day I died. That was over ten years ago."

Both aliens were pale, and their mouths hung open by the time Adam finished his tale, the one about how he had died, been brought back to life by the mutants, and then, as his body began to deteriorate, Panur cloned him a new body, complete with all his old memories. He told them about how the cloning was interrupted and how his body was still going through the process but at a much slower pace. And because his body was still regenerating, any injury he suffered healed faster and painful episodes lasted only a fraction of the time they normally would have.

When he was done, the doctors sat silent for a full minute before Simfas spoke.

"That is an incredible story, but why have you told us this? From what I can see, you are essentially healed. We can be of no further service to you."

"I want you to see if my blood—or whatever—can help Tidus."

The stunned doctors looked at each other.

"You believe your body can help heal your friend?" Klastor asked.

Adam shook his head. "I don't know if that's possible, but it's worth a try, isn't it? A blood transfusion, or even filtering out what I call my cloning juice. What do we have to lose?"

"There could be a chance that disrupting this slow-moving process may stop it completely—within you," said Simfas. "Of course, that is pure conjecture." His face slowly began to animate, realizing what an opportunity Adam was offering him. Adam had not only been brought back to life but was also cloned. Cloning wasn't unusual, but the way Adam was cloned was a miracle.

"Will you do it?" Adam asked. "Will you take whatever fluids you need from me and use them on Tidus?"

"I would be honored," said Doctor Simfas. Klastor wasn't so quick to agree.

"This could take time," Adam's doctor cautioned. "If we do isolate this so-called cloning juice, there is no guarantee it can be synthesized or that it would work on the Juirean."

"I realize that," said Adam. "But if we do nothing, Tidus could be a vegetable for the rest of his life."

The aliens recoiled. "I do not understand the reference," Klastor said.

"It means he may never recover, either to remain in the coma or eventually die. I don't want either to happen. Take what you need from me."

The doctors looked again at each other and then began strategizing. "We will have to set up a special unit to study the Human," said Simfas. "Full scans, the best chemists. If this healing agent can be isolated and synthesized, it could revolutionize medicine across the galaxy." He looked at Adam. "Mr. Cain, I am impressed with the level of devotion you have to your friend, so much so that you would sacrifice your time and your body to the pursuit of science—"

"Nah, that's not going to happen," Adam interrupted. "You can't have *me*, just my fluids. I have another mission I need to tend to. Maybe, after I'm through, you can have my body … if there's anything left of it. But for now, I'll give you two days to take whatever samples and scans you need, but then I'm gone."

Both aliens were on their feet, sensing the urgency of the matter. With the clout Simfas had, Adam was sure things would move quickly. And although he knew it was a longshot that anything in Adam's body could help Tidus, he had to try. Besides, it gave him an ounce of hope for his friend. And maybe, if the doctors had a little extra healing juice left over after curing Tidus, they could give some to Siri. It might help with her physical injuries, if not the emotional heartbreak.

Later that day, a Tel'oran police officer entered Adam's room. The Human had asked to speak with the lead investigator, and now he was here with a datapad in his hand and a frown on his face. His name was Clayus Bax, and Adam had heard of him. The bombing of the Starfire Building was the greatest act of terrorism in the planet's history, so their most renown investigator was assigned the case. Being both in the same occupation, peripherally, Clayus knew of Adam, as well.

"Before we begin," Clayus said with grave sincerity, "I have learned of your true name. There are also rumors circulating within the hospital of a special project being set up to study you. As an investigator, I must ask the question. I know it is a fantastical question, but are you the Adam Cain of Human legend? The fact that everyone is speaking of your miraculous recovery demands an answer."

Adam appreciated the police officer's candor. He had a curiosity and logical mind that Adam respected. And since Adam had no idea what lay in his future, he didn't give a damn who knew who he was at this point.

He nodded. "I am. And before you ask more, I was cloned, and that is why I look and heal the way I do."

Clayus was silent as he processed the information. Just saying one was cloned didn't fully explain Adam's younger appearance and full cognitive abilities. But that was a mystery for another time. But still ... "I researched you before attending this meeting. The names of the mutants Panur and Lila read prominently in your history, even to the point where it says Lila Bol is your daughter?"

"She is."

Clayus maintained his composure. "You helped birth the most powerful being in the known universe—from what they say, even more powerful than Panur. Is that because you are a mutant as well?"

Adam shook his head. "Unfortunately, no. I was just the culmination of an incredible three-billion-year-long experiment. The only thing that made me special is that I'm a Human who mated with a Formilian. It was a once in several billion-year occurrence. Now, can we get on to more pressing issues?"

"You wish to know who is responsible for the bombing of your building and the death of your friends," Clayus stated. "That is understandable, and from professional courtesy, I will comply, although, at this point, there is little to go on."

"Is anyone claiming responsibility?"

"Not at this point. All we know is that an experimental high-power explosive was laid at the southern footings of the building. It has been determined that if placed more strategically, the entire building could have been brought down. That led us to suspect that there was a specific target, along with considerable collateral damage to cover the act."

"The Juirean, Tidus Fe Nolan," Adam stated.

Clayus nodded. "Fortunately, he was not in his office at the time, but rather, was on the other side of the building."

"That was because he gave up the office a few days before the bombing."

The detective frowned and made a note on the datapad. "Why would he do that? Does not the timing seem suspect?"

Adam smirked. "Not at all. He just appointed a chief executive officer, and the pair traded offices. No one outside the upper echelon at Starfire knew of this."

"Why was he relinquishing control? The Juirean has been a fixture at Starfire for several years. His work ethic and devotion to the company are legendary."

Adam pursed his lips. "Believe it or not, he wanted to go into politics. I guess he wants to give something back to the community through public service."

The officer grunted and made more notes.

"Do you have any idea who did this?" the inspector asked Adam.

"You know the job we do. It could be one of a dozen or more people or factions. And you say you don't have any suspects, no ideas of your own?"

"I never said we did not have suspects. You asked if anyone claimed responsibility."

Adam sat up in the bed. "You have suspects? Who are they!"

Clayus raised a hand to calm Adam. "At the moment, they are barely suspects."

"Tell me about them."

"As I said, the explosive was experimental, and so it gives off a unique chemical signature. The two individuals we have in custody had slight—very slight—traces of this chemical on their clothing when they attempted to board a starliner off the planet. We have been questioning them for two weeks, but so far, neither has admitted to anything. It is possible they rubbed up against the package holding the explosive or they might have bumped into the true terrorists. At this point, we have no way of knowing."

Adam slipped off the bed. "Then let's go," he said to Clayus. "Let me have a crack at them."

Clayus remained seated, shaking his head. "You have no authorization; besides, there are rules as to the treatment of prisoners, let alone suspects. They have retained legal representation and are being advised not to speak further."

"Fuck that!" Adam yelled. "Just give me two minutes with them, and I'll have the answers. Inspector Clayus, this was a major afront to Tel'oran society. It calls for a little *enhanced* interrogation if you know what I mean."

"Unfortunately, I do know what you mean, and the

answer is no. You cannot physically harm the suspects, and for the past two weeks, we have asked them every question imaginable." Then he grimaced. "I will not allow you to speak to them. Besides, soon they will be released. We have no evidence to hold them longer."

Adam's jaw dropped. "You're going to let them go?"

"We have no choice. They have rights."

"When is this going to happen?"

Clayus grinned. "I am not going to tell you that. Forgive me, but I know of your reputation."

"What does that mean?" Adam asked although he knew exactly what the inspector was saying.

Clayus just smirked.

Adam climbed off the bed. "I want you to come with me."

"Where?"

"I want you to meet someone," Adam said, heading for the door.

"Who?"

"You will see. Please, Inspector, indulge me."

Reluctantly, Clayus followed Adam to Siri's hospital room.

The feline telepath perked up when she saw Adam but then frowned when she saw Clayus.

"This is Siri," Adam began. "She is a co-worker of mine who was injured in the explosion."

Clayus and Siri exchanged hostile looks.

"Yes, the Inspector and I have already met," Siri said caustically.

"I interviewed her six days ago," Clayus explained. "I am glad to see you are feeling better. As I said before, I feel your grief."

"I am sure you do," Siri growled, her eyes staring unblinkingly at the police officer.

Clayus looked to Adam. "Appealing to my sympathy will not gain you access—"

"Access to what?" Siri asked anxiously.

Adam grinned. "It seems the inspector here has a couple of suspects in custody, and he will not allow me to interview them. And beyond that, he says they're going to be released soon, but he won't tell me when."

Adam noticed the sparkling in Siri's eyes. She focused on the police officer.

"So, you have secrets, Inspector Clayus," Siri said wickedly.

"They are not so much secrets as privileged information. There are protocols. You both are in the security business; you know there are rules and procedures."

As he spoke, Clayus was becoming nervous. He could see the amusement on the faces of the two Starfire employees, and it made him uncomfortable.

"I do not see the significance of this meeting," he stammered. "Now, Adam Cain, I must admit to some shock at learning your true identity, but even in light of that—perhaps because of that—I must now take my leave.

Any further information we discover will be passed along once it has been cleared by my office. Other than that, I respectfully request that you maintain your distance from the investigation and let Tel'oran authorities do our job."

"When and where are you releasing the prisoners?" Adam asked out of the blue.

Clayus blinked and recoiled slightly. "Have you not heard a word I said?"

"I did," Adam replied with a grin. "I just want to make sure you know when and where they'll be released."

Clayus again shook his head. "Of course, I know. And that is the way it shall remain. Now, this conversation has become … strange. I will be leaving now."

He bowed awkwardly and then left the room. Adam looked at Siri, who smiled broadly at him.

"I got it. Two days from now, Day-16, the South Entrance to the main police headquarters. I even have a mental description."

"Charlie…"

Adam's ATD allowed Siri access to Adam's brain, where she transferred the mental image of the suspects she had scanned from the inspector's mind. It was all quite spooky and supernatural but efficient.

"I will be there," Siri stated seriously.

Adam nodded. "I'll make the arrangements." He patted her shoulder. "Get some rest. I'll see you in two days."

6

Adam was dressed in a standard white cabbie jacket, leaning against the black transport in the bright sunshine of early afternoon two days later. He had come early and reserved one of the rare parking spaces near the South Entrance to the police building. Feigning boredom, he kept looking at his watch as Day-16 approached.

Several other drivers gave him nasty looks as he hogged the parking space, but he just shrugged them off. He wanted to make sure he was the first transport the suspects saw as they stepped out of the building. Even so, he had a plan in mind.

Twenty minutes after the appointed hour, the pair of aliens pressed through the exit door, trailing a set of wheeled luggage cases with them. They had been preparing to board a starship when they were detained. Now, they were anxious to resume their journey.

Adam spotted them immediately and began waving his arm impatiently. The aliens—each non-Tel'oran—looked at him questioningly. But still, they approached.

"It is about time," Adam said with disgust. "I have been waiting here for nearly two hours." He stepped up to them and took their cases, moving them to the rear trunk.

"Who are you?" the shorter of the two asked, a creature even shorter than Adam and with a frog's face. His eyes were narrow and keen, obviously the leader of the pair. The other alien was tall and slender, with pinkish skin and bony plates that flared back from his head, and he had serious dreadlocks that reached the pit of his back.

"I am Boris," Adam said, pulling the name out of nowhere. "I've been sent to take you to the spaceport. Now, hurry, or else you will miss your connection."

"Who sent you?"

Adam opened the back door, and Dreadlocks climbed in. Frogface hesitated.

"I work for a service," Adam replied. "That's all I know. They don't tell me who we contract with. Now, are you coming?" He looked at his watch. "I was told your flight lifts at Day-20, and there is a lot of traffic between here and the spaceport."

With a defiant grunt, Frogface climbed in the back.

The transport was a legitimate limousine of Tel'oran design. Adam knew a guy who knew a guy who let him rent it for the afternoon. Adam moved around to the driver's side and climbed in.

"There are drinks in the side doors if you are interested. It's a hot one here today. Been like this all week."

Looking at the rear seat camera screen, Adam saw that Dreadlocks was already scanning the selection. He chose an intoxicant. Frogface was still more cautious, looking out the window as the limo pulled away from the parking spot, which was immediately taken by another cab. Adam merged with traffic as Frogface pulled a water bottle from the offered menu.

Adam relaxed, displaying a slight grin. It would only take a moment …

Xapin looked at his companion, a question on his face.

"Who was that?"

"I know not," said Porison. "We are to make sure they go to the spaceport without contact or deviation. We will follow to make sure that happens."

Xapin engaged the transport, and it moved out into traffic, following the long, black vehicle. "Let Salwan know that they have left the police facility."

Porison nodded and made the link.

By the time Adam was a mile from the police station, both his occupants were knocked out on the backseat, having drank the tranquilizer. It didn't matter which bottle they drank from; they were all spiked. Another three miles later, Adam turned off the main road and entered the warehouse district of Dal Innis.

The arrangements he'd made didn't have to be elaborate, just a quiet place where he and Siri could 'interview' the suspects. With Siri's talent, it would only take seconds to know if they were guilty. If they were innocent, Adam would drop them on a curb somewhere outside the gates of the spaceport. If they were guilty, well, that was another story.

The door to the warehouse was open, and Adam drove in. It closed automatically using Adam's ATD. Only a few overhead lights lit the cold, open space, looking gothic and noir. Two chairs were placed side by side in the middle of the room, with another for Adam. Siri was in a wheelchair, a traction brace on her leg and her left arm strapped across her chest. She still had bandages on the side of her face.

Her face twisted in agony as Adam helped her into the wheelchair at the hospital, but she didn't complain. The nursing staff protested vehemently but then went surprisingly silent, their eyes vacant, as Siri glanced at them. Siri was both a telepath and a null. She could read minds as well as effect emotions. It was a handy trick to have, and Adam wished he had it himself. Instead, he had Charlie, which was pretty awesome in its own right.

Adam was late, according to Siri's accounting, and she displayed it on her face.

"Any problems?" she asked as Adam climbed out of the car.

"No; it just took longer in central processing. Nothing to worry about."

He moved to the back of the car and carried the aliens to the chairs. They were strapped to the armrest and their ankles bound. Once they were secure, Adam returned to the car. "Let me get the antidote—"

"Do not bother," Siri said cryptically.

Adam turned in time to see the two aliens suddenly spasm awake, their eyes bulging, their mouths open. A little mental wake-up call, Adam reasoned.

After regaining their senses, each alien looked around, scanning their surroundings. Dreadlocks had a look of sheer terror on his face, while Froggie was more in control. He frowned, looking at Siri's injuries, but then pursed his wide lips, sensing what this was about.

Adam sat down in the chair. This was Siri's show, and the Human was just along for the ride.

"I will get right to the point," Siri purred ominously. Her soft and narrow feline features were deceiving, but when she snarled, displaying needle-sharp teeth, both aliens recoiled slightly. "Did you bomb the Starfire Building?"

"Of course not," Dreadlocks said in a yell. "We have

been asked that for days now. How many times do we need to repeat ourselves?"

Siri focused on Froggie. He met her gaze with defiance.

"Calm yourself, Greken," he said in a baritone voice. "These two already believe they know the truth."

"They are wrong!" Greken replied.

"I know they are. However, where the police used logic and protocol, these two believe they are above the law. Remain calm. The worst they can do is kill us."

"But we have done nothing wrong," Greken countered.

"I am done playing with you," Siri stated. She looked at Dreadlocks. His face went suddenly blank, his nervous fidgeting ending. "Did you bomb the Starfire Building?"

"Yes," Greken stated flatly.

Froggie jerked his head at his companion. "Silence! She is using some kind of hypnosis on you, getting you to say what she wants you to say."

Siri smiled. "Is that so?" Froggie's face went blank. "Did you bomb the Starfire Building?"

"Yes," came the instant reply.

Siri mentally released the prisoners. It was much more fun when they knew they had no way of hiding the truth from her.

Both aliens looked at her before Froggie took the lead again.

"This is coercion! This is not legal. You made us say that."

Siri nodded. "I did. I made you tell the truth. And you should be aware I can do a lot more than just that."

Dreadlocks suddenly released a bloodcurdling scream that echoed throughout the empty warehouse. Froggie pulled away from him, terror on his face. Greken regained his composure ... to a degree. His breath still came in fits, and his eyes bulged.

"What happened?" Froggie asked.

"I ... I do not know," Greken answered. "I was suddenly in a burning pit of liquid, my flesh boiling from my bones." He was staring at Siri, terror burning in his eyes.

"See, I can do anything I want with you mentally. I could easily enter your brains and extract every memory of your horrific deed. I can plant visions and emotions in you of the pain and sorrow I feel with the loss of my unborn child and my mated, I can do all that, and more. But now, I want you to tell me the truth, all the truth, and without prompting. I want you to confess to me how you destroyed half a building and killed hundreds of my friends and colleagues. And then I want you to tell me why and who you are working for. Do that, and I will let you die with dignity. Resist, and I will send you down the *Pit of Fanosh*, which is my people's version of Hell. I will leave you there to suffer for—"

"We were hired by Salwan Saif," Froggie blurted

before Siri could finish her threat. She was disappointed; she was just coming to the best part.

"Who is Salwan Saif?" Adam asked.

"He is a dealer in stolen energy modules on the planet Ropor."

Adam had never heard the name before. "Why would he want the building bombed?"

Froggie shook his head. "I do not know. We were paid two hundred thousand energy credits for the job. We did not ask why. One does not ask why in our business."

"Did you work alone on Tel'oran?"

"No, we received the explosive from a contact. We are demolition experts. We were tasked with determining the best place to set the explosives. We did that two days before the devices were detonated. We did not initiate the explosions. That was done remotely. We were to remain on the planet to make sure all traces were covered."

"Who pressed the button?" Adam asked.

Froggie shook his head. "I do not know. We were given the detonators, and that was it. They could have been triggered from anywhere in the galaxy."

"Who gave you the explosives?" Siri asked.

Froggie jumped when she spoke, having had his concentration on Adam. Adam thought it was amusing; he was usually the one people were afraid of. In this case, it was Siri.

"I have no names; again, that is how it is done. We

were told to go to an address, and there we found the items."

"What was the address?"

"I ... I cannot remember. We are not of Tel'oran, and we only went there once."

Dreadlocks suddenly writhed with pain, his eyes manic, and his long tongue lashing across his face. Then he fell silent again. Froggie looked at Siri with stark, unbridled fear in his eyes.

"It is an address on Jerplin Causeway," Siri told Adam.

Froggie's eyes grew wider, seeing again the depth of Siri's powers. "I have told you the truth, all that I know!"

"No, you haven't," Adam said. "Tell us more about Salwan Saif. Where is his headquarters, and how big is his operation?"

"His operation, as I said, is on Ropor, the settlement of Lan Morif. He is very powerful there. That is where we come from. We have done work for him before. As I said, we are demolition experts."

"So, he's blown-up buildings before?" Siri asked.

"He has blown up many things, but mainly starships. A building is easy. It is stationary—"

Froggie's face suddenly contorted, becoming a Pablo Picasso version of itself. Adam placed a calming hand on Siri's shoulder. "Later, we still need a little more information."

Froggie gasped, and his head fell forward. It took him several seconds to recover.

"Go on," Adam began. "Tell us about his organization."

"He has many soldiers and operates throughout the Darius Branch. Do you know where that is?"

Adam nodded.

"His primary business is stealing energy pods and reselling them, but that is only part of his operation. I do not know its full extent."

"Is he part of a larger organization?"

"I believe so; most operations such as his are. They survive only by the grace of someone more powerful."

"Do you know who?" Adam asked.

Froggie shook his huge, round head. "I do not. We are low-level soldiers, specialists. We only do what we are paid to do."

Adam leaned back in the chair, thinking if he had enough information from these two. Unfortunately for them, he believed he did. He nodded to Siri.

Froggie and Graken began bouncing with fear, the legs of their metal chairs squeaking on the concrete floor.

"We have cooperated!" Froggie cried out, sensing what was coming. "Please spare us!"

"I will," Siri said, surprisingly. Adam looked at her, not knowing where this was going. "If you can honestly tell me you have remorse for what you have done, what you have done to me!"

"Yes, yes!" the aliens blathered. "We are so terribly sorry. Please, please forgive us."

Then Graken went null again. Froggie looked at him with shock.

"Do you have remorse for what you have done?" Siri asked Dreadlocks.

"No," came the emotionless answer.

Froggie didn't know what to do. "That ... that is him. I do have remorse! Honestly."

"Really?" Siri asked with a sinister grin. "You know you can hide nothing from me. No matter what you say to my face, I can find your true emotions. Now, I will ask you again: Do you have any remorse for killing my friends, my mate and my unborn daughter?"

Froggie's face suddenly went hard and defiant. He knew his cause was lost.

"No, I have no remorse for what I have done," he admitted. "I know not of you or anyone else on this planet, so why should I care? Salwan wanted the building to come down, and that is what we did. We have killed hundreds more. You, and the lives of your loved ones, mean nothing to me."

Siri did her best to lean in closer to Froggie, but her traction gear would not allow her to do so. She relaxed back and then met the alien's eyes. "Then I will make you suffer the most. And throughout it all, you will know that I, too, care nothing for you or how much you suffer."

Adam didn't ask what Siri did to their minds; he wouldn't understand even if she told him. Instead, he watched with detached amusement as their eyes began to waiver and their faces contorted. Bodies quivered uncontrollably, and they both toppled sideways, taking the chairs with them.

"Let us go," Siri said to Adam. "I am done here."

"What about them?"

"They will last as long as their bodies hold out, maybe a few hours, maybe a day. The longer, the better."

Adam stepped behind the wheelchair and moved Siri to the car. It was a chore getting her inside before folding the wheelchair and placing it in the truck. He left the killers' luggage on the floor of the deserted warehouse.

"There!" said Porison, watching as a roll-up door down the alley opened and a long, black transport pulled out. The vehicle turned in their direction down the lane. Xapin had a long-range camera lens hooked above the window, and he made detailed recordings of the two occupants as they drove by no more than fifty feet away.

Xapin checked the camera file.

"I do not see Graken and Quanis. And now there is a female in the vehicle." He scanned the images again before transmitting them to his counterparts.

"We will know who they are soon," he said to his partner. "Now, let us go to the warehouse."

They drove the short distance to the designated building. The door was closed, meaning either someone was still inside or it was on a remote control. Porison got out of the transport and tried a side door. It was locked, but not for long. Porison was a brute of a creature, and he was able to break the latch with ease.

The lights were still on inside the empty cavernous room ... empty except for the two writhing and screaming bodies strapped to chairs. Xapin and Porison ran to them. They did not know the pair, having only seen them at the police station and from a distance as the demolition experts came to retrieve the bombs and triggers. But still, they were of the same fraternity.

They were cut from the armrests, but the two gangsters kept their legs bound. The two off-worlders were in the throes of some kind of spastic fit and were a danger not only to themselves but others. The pair of Tel'orans stood back, watching and waiting until others arrived. What had happened here was above their grade level. Others would have to decide what to do with the screaming bombers. But whatever had happened, it did not bode well for the secrecy of the operation. The two aliens in the transport had gotten what they wanted—that was obvious—and then left the bombers to suffer their anguished fate, perhaps by a poison of some kind. What that meant for Xapin and Porison and the rest of the Tel'oran contingent, well, that was still to be determined.

7

Siri was an emotional wreck when Adam left her at the hospital. She wanted to come with him on his mission of retribution, but physically, she wasn't up to it. Honestly, Adam would have loved to have her with him. Together, they made a lethal team. Adam particularly liked her idea of long-term mind-fucking the bad guys. But since she couldn't come with him, and he didn't have her skills, he would have to settle for some old-fashioned brute force retribution.

And to that end, the next stop Adam made was to his storage locker located just outside the gates of the Executive Spaceport where the *Arieel* was berthed. He opened the steel container and turned on the lights. Stacks of crates lined the fifteen-foot-high side walls, along with cases of metal drawers against the back. This was where Adam kept his store of weapons, explosives and other accouterments of his trade, be it either as a bounty hunter, bodyguard or mercenary. Not everything would fit in the *Arieel*, nor was it wise to journey across the galaxy from one hostile center to another with so much loose firepower aboard. He'd collected the items essentially over a lifetime of galactic 'wet work,' and it was here where Adam kept his cache of Human weapons. Flash weapons were okay in certain circumstances, but this time, Adam wasn't messing around. He wanted some serious firepower, and nothing but kinetic weapons from good ol' Mother Earth would do.

He had Glocks, SIG Sauers, S&Ws ... just about every make of handgun imaginable. And then he had sniper rifles: a McMillian Tac-50, an M82 SASR, along with Remingtons and H&K. Most of these were a collection more than actual armament, having been replaced by newer versions over the years. But since Adam had no intention of making long-distance shots, he only took one, an H&K M220, which was only five years old.

His main concern was ammunition. The advantage flash weapons had over kinetic was they could be easily recharged anywhere. But finding the proper rounds for his Human weapons was the challenge. And that's why he'd stockpiled his supply over the years. He estimated he had over a quarter million rounds of a variety of calibers in his storeroom. He did know how to load himself, but that took time and precision. Instead, he chose just to keep buying more readymade ammo stock when he could.

Now, he began to load boxes and ammo cases full of nine-millimeter, .45, 308, 7.62 and more. He took shoulder, waist, ankle and back holsters. He took Tasers and modern projection swords that could generate a two-thousand-degree temperature along the edges. He took diffusion shields, electronic surveillance and comm systems, night vision goggles and contact lenses. He took monoscopes ... frankly, everything and anything he imagined he might need.

As far as he knew, he was going after a single person, someone named Salwan Saif. But it was the screen of security personnel he might have around him that Adam had to be concerned with. Then, there was the question of what type of statement he wanted to make. Simply getting revenge may sound sweet, but what would that do in the long run? At the moment, Adam didn't know. All he knew was he had a seething anger burning inside him. He had had loss in his life, horrible, traumatic loss, when his wife Maria and daughter Cassie were killed in the first Juirean firebombing of Earth. That was so long ago, and he'd tried desperately to bury those feelings.

But in reality, it was that anger that had sustained him for so long. The aliens did this to him, to his family, to his people. And Humanity never asked for any of this to happen to them. Earth could have gone on for a thousand years before developing a gravity drive of its own. Then, mankind would have stepped into the world of the Juireans and the Klin. That would have been our doing ... but at that time. Instead, the galaxy, along with all its fucked-up politics, was foisted upon the Human race whether they wanted it or not.

Surprisingly, humanity responded in kind to the horror and atrocities it suffered. Perhaps the change was inevitable as the race melded with the galaxy as a whole. But if left alone, we would have had hundreds of years of innocence before that happened.

However, the aliens wouldn't leave us alone. And they paid the price for messing with the Humans.

Recently, Adam Cain had come to accept the alien world as his own. He hadn't been to Earth in eight years, and that was only briefly. Now, he felt comfortable on Tel'oran, enough to let a small group of aliens into his inner circle. He truly cared for Siri and Vinset. And especially Tidus. Sure, they jousted now and then, but it was all in good fun. And the fact that he was a Juirean made the bond between them even more unusual—and special.

And now his friend lay hooked to a respirator and probably will be for the rest of his short life. It was too early to tell if Adam's magnanimous gesture with his bodily fluids would help or not.

And then there was Vinset. If ever there was a stand-up guy—for an alien—it was him. He'd saved Adam's life a couple of times, and Adam returned the favor just as many. They were two peas-in-a-pods, although Vinset was much more honorable. Damn, Adam was going to miss him.

And then came Siri.

Because of her 'disability' of being a mutant, she was an outcast on her homeworld, forcing her to roam the space lanes, making a living as best she could. She, too, didn't ask to be different. And although she may have done some bad things in the past, it wasn't how she was inside. She was pragmatic, and pragmatic people do what must be done to survive. Recently, however, she'd found her calling working for Starfire. With the company, she felt she was on the side of good, the side of justice. She thrived in that environment.

And then she found true love with Vinset. Adam acknowledged that it seemed strange that members of two different species would be so attracted to one another, but Adam felt the same ... about Arieel. It was just how these things went. And then to take the step to become a mother, with Vinset accepting the role of father to a child that was not of his race. It spoke volumes about both of them.

And then there were the others, so many others, who now lay either in hospital beds or in the morgue. They didn't deserve any of this. They were the infamous collateral damage that seemed to follow Adam everywhere he went, although in this case, he wasn't the cause of the catastrophe.

Or was he? So far, he didn't know for sure. He had no idea who Salwan Saif was and whether or not he was the one who ultimately ordered the bombing. But he was a good place to start.

As Adam loaded four crates of weapons, gear, and ammo into the transport, he was still unclear about his mission. Was he out to get justice by killing the person responsible for the deaths and destruction? Or was he out to crush the organization that spawned and supported such people? At the moment, he didn't care which. All he wanted was to destroy, to turn order into chaos, what the scientists called entropy.

In the shadows of the approaching night on Tel'oran, Adam began to chant a saying in his mind. It would be his mantra as he went forth, his clarion call.

"I am entropy," he said aloud. "I will bring chaos to order. I will bring it all crashing down … or I will die trying."

8

The warehouse was filled with six other beings, mainly Tel'oran, plus Porison and Xapin. The leader, an alien named Rafis, had been running the local cell for several months, and Xapin had learned not to question his orders. He had no feelings, no concern for others, only the mission. And now he stood looking dispassionately at the still writhing creatures on the floor. Their whimpering had quieted some, mainly because they were running out of energy. They lay in pools of sweat and urine and smelled horrendous.

"What is wrong with them?" Rafis asked the medical expert who had come in response to the reports by the two scouts. With the help of the others, the patients were restrained long enough for a quick examination.

"I do not know," said the doctor. "They appear to be suffering some cognitive disorder, almost like a waking terror. They are unresponsive to outside stimuli. I did a blood test, and neither have drugs in their systems that would cause this. But, in my opinion, they are lost in whatever horror they are experiencing."

Rafis grunted, pulled out an MK-88 and placed a bolt in each of their heads, ending the wailing and gyrations. The rest of the people in the warehouse were relieved. The pair of insane operatives were making them nervous. Although they'd never worked directly with the bombers, to see a pair of their comrades-in-arms so thoroughly incapacitated—to the point of on-going torture—was unsettling.

Rafi then turned his attention to the two scouts, focusing on Xapin. "How long were they in the room before they left?"

"Not more than ten minutes."

"And you believe that was long enough to extract information from them?"

"They did not know they were being followed; therefore, they had all the time they needed."

"You believe the bombers revealed our secrets?"

Xapin was going out on a limb, but it was the only way he was going to advance in the organization, by showing initiative and decisiveness.

"Yes, I do. Why leave otherwise? They obviously had the means of affecting Graken and Quanis's minds. They would only leave them as they did if the bombers were of no further use to them."

Rafis looked to the doctor.

"It could be a form of induced hypnosis, although without the use of chemicals," he concurred. "It can be done."

"And it could leave them in such a state?"

"It is possible," the doctor replied. "I do not know how, but these are two aliens. I know not what skills they possess."

Rafis turned to another of his entourage. "Do we have an identity yet?"

The Tel'oran was working his datapad. "It is coming through now."

"Open a link with Ropor. We must share this information immediately. If our cell has been compromised, steps must be taken to mitigate the damage."

Three hundred forty light years away, Salwan Saif studied the images on the screen just beamed to him from Tel'oran. His aide studied them on another screen in the office while also working a computer.

"They are both employees of Starfire Security," said Laz'morin Nawnic, a trim-looking creature with black skin and grey eyes that seemed to blaze on the smooth face. "The male is identified simply as *The Human*."

"I recognize the species," said Salwan. He was a shorter creature with yellow-tinged skin, two large eyes and a pair of sensor feelers on his forehead. He was a Val'

Graf with frog-like legs and muscular arms of incredible strength. He relished his advantage over nearly all around him, hosting boxing and wrestling exhibitions between him and his staff. He always won, which was expected.

Being attuned to his unnatural strength, he was acutely aware of the Human race. For fifty standard years, it was their strength, coordination and tenacity that provided much of their legend. Although Salwan had never fought a Human before; however, he would consider them a worthy adversary, if ever the opportunity arose for a contest. A contest under his control and supervision, of course. Salwan was egotistical, but he wasn't stupid.

"And the female?" he asked Laz'morin.

"She is called Siri and is also an operative. She is a creature with no special attributes, as far as we can tell."

"Her attributes—as well as that of the Human—is that they both survived the explosion."

"Many others did, as well," Laz'morin reminded Salwan. "The mission was not to bring down the entire building, only a portion of it."

"Which could prove to have been a mistake on our part." He turned to another screen on the wall, one that displayed a bare concrete warehouse an unimaginable distance away. "You believe these two may have extracted information from our agents?"

"I do," Rafis said from Tel'oran. "And even if they have not, they are undertaking an active investigation beyond the scope of local law enforcement. What they did here would not be tolerated otherwise."

"They are a danger to us," Salwan summarized.

Rafis nodded.

"Then deal with them. Keep it quiet if you can, but hurry. We cannot let any information they may have filter beyond them. Use whatever assets you require."

Again, Rafis nodded, but this time with a glint in his eyes. Salwan cut the link.

9

Siri was having trouble getting comfortable. Her arm was out of traction, but her leg was still bound and held in place. Without let up, the nurses and doctors had complained about her leaving the hospital, and now they said they felt no sympathy for how she was feeling. It was her own fault.

Eventually, she was given a sleeping potion, which helped her drift off. But now her dreams were filled with nightmarish images of things she couldn't have possibly witnessed: Vinset falling through the air as the building below him crumbled, along with the suffocating screams of her still barely-formed child. But in her vision, her daughter was fully formed, beautiful and full of promise. And then, the next moment, she was gone.

Siri had a very special mind, and although she knew the images weren't real, she almost thought of them as projections through time and space to real events. Even in her sleep, she tried to rationalize her dreams. She was a part of them but separate, aware that she was dreaming but unable to change the outcome. In every horrific scenario, Vinset and her child died.

And then she felt a familiar tingling, something those of her race called *the itch*. Being as sensitive to their surroundings as they were, they could sense changes in air pressure and temperature. This had nothing to do with Siri's unusual mental abilities but was instinctive to her race. There were people in her room, and more than one.

With a strange sense of regret, Siri abandoned her nightmarish dreams for reality. She didn't need to open her eyes to track the intruders if they really were intruders. That was a problem for her. Every time a nurse entered her room, she would wake up. It wasn't the nurse's fault, but it always took a while for her to fall off to sleep again.

But this was different. These were males—she could smell them. And there were three of them, meaning they weren't orderlies or doctors. One had moved to the right side of the bed, while the other two approached from the left, near the entrance.

Siri wasn't afraid because, in an instant, she was inside their minds without them knowing it. But what she saw there was horrifying. They had come to kill her.

Her eyes flew open the instant she locked the three killers in place. The shocked looks on their faces were frozen in place as they became aware that their target was awake and that their bodies couldn't move. Panic filled their eyes as Siri probed, learning that they had all been in the warehouse earlier and seen their comrades writhing in pain and insanity. Is this how the mental torture started, they questioned in their confused thoughts.

"Yes, it is," Siri confirmed as she pressed herself painfully into a sitting position. "This is what happened to your friends," she said in an ominous trill. "But you can be relieved that that will not happen to you."

Her words brought no comfort to the terrified looks of the would-be killers.

Siri continued. "That is because I do not have the time to play with you. Now, let me probe deeper. What else do you know besides my identity?"

As feared, they had a full workup on Adam, but they knew him only as The Human. They had his location, being that of the *Arieel* at the Executive Spaceport. And there was a team heading to him, as well.

And with that knowledge, Siri simply snapped the fingers on her good left hand. All three natives collapsed to the floor, dead from massive cerebral hemorrhages.

She left the bodies lying there as she struggled to get the communicator off the nightstand. It was a reach, and she nearly fell off the bed, trying to reach it. Then she punched in Adam's number. The connection beeped at her several times—too many times. She broke the connection and tried again. Still nothing.

And then her vivid imagination—or was it prescience

—kicked in again, this time showing the dimly lit area around the *Arieel* with a scattering of bodies lying about. Panic set in. Was Adam included in the dead? She squeezed her eyes shut, refusing to see the rest of the vision, afraid it was a version of the truth her imagination was creating. In her present state of mind, there was no telling what horrors her mind would produce.

Heads up, Adam, said Charlie in his mind. *There are weapons surrounding your position.*

Adam was outside the *Arieel*, moving the crates into the cargo hold, enjoying the relative coolness of the early evening after an exceptionally warm day in Dal Innis. His mind was still cluttered with all the what-ifs of his diaphanous mission, trying to bring form to it. But now Charlie alerted him to a threat. And it had to be a threat for his ATD to warn him. Just about everyone on Tel'oran carried an energy weapon, so detecting them in the area wasn't unusual. But detecting a circle moving around the *Arieel* was grounds for alarm.

Charlie projected a heads-up-display into Adam's mind, highlighting the locations of the intruders. He was afraid something like this might happen, although he knew the gangsters at the warehouse hadn't informed on him and Siri. He had to have been followed from the police station. He grimaced. That was his fault. He should have been more careful.

Charlie, link with Siri's room phone and tell her to be aware. It looks as if I might be busy for a few minutes.

Adam wasn't worried about Siri. It took a lot to sneak up on her, even if she was in a deep sleep. He grimaced slightly. She wouldn't be playing around this time.

There were ten of them, and each with two weapons. All Adam saw in his mind were white dots projected on his vision. They came in pairs, two pairs coming around the far side of the *Arieel* and three pairs coming from the roadway. They were moving in the shadows and behind other ships. Adam lived in the storage section of the spaceport, which was more crowded than out on the flight line. The ships here were towed to the large field before activating their engines. Adam essentially lived in a trailer park of starships.

The Human wasn't overly worried. Charlie had already disabled the twenty energy weapons. That would have been difficult for him to do if they had all come in shooting. But with their cautious approach, he had plenty of time. Now, Adam lifted the lid of the crate he had been moving into the ship and reached in, removing two SIG Sauer nine millimeters and stuffing them into his waist belt. There was a box of magazines buried a little deeper. He rummaged through the crate until he found it. Then he stuffed three mags into each of his pockets while inserting loaded magazines into the weapons. He pulled back the slides, arming the weapons.

He was in no mood to play. He knew who was behind

this, so the attackers had no information he needed. His ship was loaded and ready to go, so let Inspector Clayus sort out the carnage after he was gone. He didn't care.

Nonchalantly, Adam turned toward the closest pair, a SIG Sauer held in each hand. Although he wanted to simply blast into the dark, he still had to be sure this was an attacking force and not just a bunch of his friends playing a joke on him. Of course, most of his friends on Tel'oran were either injured or dead. Still, a little caution was called for.

He stood in plain sight as a pair of attackers lifted their weapons and pulled the triggers. That was confirmation enough. Adam didn't give them the customary time to gawk at their inert weapons before he lifted the handgun in his right hand and let off with a series of quick shots that disturbed the relative quiet of the spaceport. The spaceport was never quiet, not with all the take-offs and landings. But this was a new sound no one was used to, especially the attackers.

Two quick shots to the chest, then one to the head—the Mozambique Drill. Adam was deadly accurate as he stalked forward, now shifting his aim to another pair of assailants. After he Mozambiqued these two, the others got the message. But they didn't give up. Instead, they took cover. There was an odd silence around the *Arieel* as the hoods fought desperately to get their MKs working again. Adam heard power packs being dropped and new ones inserted but to no avail.

Adam casually walked up to hiding places and put caps into another two gangsters. That left four of them.

Two ran off into the dark. Adam took careful aim in the intermittent light and, at about sixty yards, placed two shots into their backs in rapid succession. He figured he needed the practice. It had been a while since he fired kinetic weapons. Damn, it felt good; his muscle memory was fully engaged.

Seeing no other escape, the last two attackers rushed at him, using their now useless weapons as cudgels. Before they reached him, Adam placed the handguns back in the waist of his pants and squared up against the aliens. He didn't have to fight them hand-to-hand, but he still had the primal urge to break something. It might as well be a couple of alien skulls.

As usual, the aliens were taller than him, and they ran with surprising quickness. Their momentum would be enough to knock Adam off his feet if he let them hit him, so at the last moment, he expertly shifted to one side and extended a leg. One assailant tripped over his leg while Adam grabbed the arm of the other as he flipped over the Human's side. Still holding the arm, Adam stepped over the attacking native on the ground and placed his shoe on the attacker's neck. He pulled on the arm and twisted at the same time. Both the neck and shoulder snapped simultaneously, killing the native instantly.

The other one was climbing back to his feet. He'd taken a nasty fall to his face after tripping over Adam's leg.

The right side of his face was bloody, and he sneered at Adam, raising his fists in what Adam guessed was a fighter's pose, at least the native Tel'oran version of one.

His anger still not satiated, Adam stepped forward, moving expertly and swiftly from side to side, moving within the range of the attacker before sweeping his right arm from left to right, blocking away the alien's weak defense. Then he came even closer before launching a swift right jab to the creature's exposed face. This was the most satisfying moment of the fight, as Adam held back none of his overwhelming Human strength. The alien's skull collapsed inward a good three inches, bathing Adam's clenched fist in blood, bone and sinew. There was even a little gray matter included.

Unfortunately, the alien was still standing, not having time to fall. Adam now unleased a left cross that impacted the still intact half of the native's face. By the time the body hit the tarmac, there wasn't much left of the head.

Adam flicked the gunk off his fists and wiped the rest on his pants. He had to say, the physical activity was more satisfying than the target shooting from earlier. He scanned around the spaceport, looking for any other potential targets. There were none, although a handful of people had appeared, drawn by the sound of incredible booms coming from his nine-millimeter. Frightened eyes looked at Adam, even from those of his regular neighbors. They knew what Adam did for a living, but after tonight, they would probably be asking for new parking space assignments, a little farther from the crazy Human and his equally crazy enemies.

Adam hastily moved the last crate into the *Arieel* and then buttoned up the hatch. As he did so, he linked mentally with Siri's room at the hospital.

"Are you okay?" she asked in a panic as Charlie made the connection.

"Yeah, I'm fine," he answered.

Adam moved to the front of the *Arieel* and attached a hook to the transport drone sitting at the front of the starship. The device activated and began towing the ship toward the flight line. Adam hustled back to the open side hatchway and sprinted to the bridge. There would be spaceport police—and others—rushing to the scene. He wanted to be off the planet before they got there. Too many questions to answer, and now that the bad guys knew Adam and Siri were on their trail, he didn't have time for them to make another attempt on his life on Tel'oran. Perhaps it was only locals who thought they would be in danger. Would Salwan Saif also be altered?

"How are you?" Adam asked Siri through the link.

"I, too, am well. There were three of them."

"Dead, I assume."

"Yes. I have not notified the hospital staff yet. I wanted to hear from you first."

"They sent a little larger team after me, but they're all

dead, too. I'm taxiing out to leave the planet as we speak. I'm sorry about having to leave you to deal with Inspector Clayus on your own. Tell him what you have to, but don't give him Salwan's name. I want him for myself."

"I understand," Siri said. There was sadness in her voice, an inevitability. "Please be careful. I know what you are planning."

"I'm planning on killing everyone and then coming home."

"Make sure you do the last part. Do not feel you need to sacrifice yourself on our behalf. Your safe return will be our greatest reward."

There was a strange void in Adam's mind. He wanted to reassure her, but he also felt numb about the prospect of him dying on the mission. If that's what happened, then so be it. This was now beyond him. But still, he played the part.

"I promise I'll be careful. I'll duck when I have to and only kill the people who deserve it."

Siri forced a laugh. "Good. Now, go, but keep me informed. Do not leave me guessing. I want to know everything you do."

"Everything?"

"Everything."

"Well, right now, I'm going to get the *Arieel* into space and then take a shower. I'm covered in blood ... someone else's blood," he amended quickly.

Siri snorted. "I figured as much."

10

"Salwan is on the link," Somick Vawsin said.

Davos Pannel crossed to the desk and punched a connecting button. A screen on the right wall came to life, showing a life-size image of a room with several aliens in it, all appearing confused. They immediately settled down when they noticed Davos on the matching screen on the planet Ropor.

Salwan Saif turned to the screen, even as an assistant was still feeding him information in his ear.

"What is happening on Tel'oran?" Davos asked forcefully, bringing everyone in the room ninety-six light-years away to instant silence.

"We are still receiving reports," Salwan answered hastily. "But it appears there have been some casualties."

Davos stared down at his associate. "Casualties? You

call fifteen dead *some* casualties. Is that not half of your force on Tel'oran?"

Salwan stopped fidgeting with his datapad, not surprised that Davos would have more information than he did about the affairs taking place on a world many light-years from both their headquarters. "Yes, fifteen have died."

"Explain what happened," Davos ordered.

"There was a possible leak of information from the bombers I sent to Tel'oran. A pair of Starfire survivors may have learned about the origins of the attack. I was attempting to seal that leak when the situation got out of hand."

"Two Starfire agents did that much damage?"

"Apparently."

Davos looked at a datapad of his own. "A single male and a female in a traction brace. How do you explain that?"

Salwan clenched his jaw in anger. "Why do you ask questions when you already know the answers?"

"I am only seeking understanding. Yes, I know what happened. I want to know *why*."

"I have no explanation at this time. None of my people survived to give a report."

"Perhaps then, I can inform you," Davos said ominously. "Yes, a female who barely survived the bombing and is still under medical care. What her involvement is, we still have not determined. However, I do have information on the male."

"Yes, he is referred to as *The Human*. He is Starfire's top agent."

"And should that have not given you pause?"

"Pause?" Salwan questioned. "They interrogated the bombers. That could lead directly to me—and, as a consequence—to you."

"I gave you the task; I did not plan the operation."

"The operation was handled flawlessly," Salwan defended. "I did just as you asked. It was never our intention to kill all Starfire agents. That would have been impossible."

"Unfortunately, the wrong one survived."

"The Human?" Salwan questioned. "Of course, but he is one agent. The next time, I will send more soldiers against him."

Davos walked closer to the screen, appearing to be almost in the same room as Salwan. He shook his head. "You will do nothing of the kind."

"Am I being punished?" Salwan asked, his anger getting the best of him. "I followed your instructions. I only did what you told me to do."

Davos grinned. "It is not what you did that has me angered; it is who you did it to."

"The Human?" Salwan gasped. "What was I supposed to do? He was coming for me."

"Do you not know who he is?"

"I told you who he is. He will be no challenge."

"Fifteen dead say otherwise."

"That is because he was underestimated. I will not do that again."

"As I said, you will do nothing!" Davos barked, causing Salwan to recoil. Then the huge syndicate boss calmed down and lifted his datapad. "Let me tell you a little about this Human creature: Two hundred eighteen class-one fugitive apprehensions in ten standard years, along with nine successful mercenary campaigns."

"Yes, his record is impressive—" Salwan conceded.

"I am not through," Davos interrupted. "Do you know the name Adam Cain?"

Salwan recoiled again from the non sequitur. "Yes, of course. Who has not heard of him?" Then Salwan nodded, gaining understanding. "He, too, was a Human, and I acknowledge that Humans are formidable opponents."

"What if I were to tell you that the Human you targeted is none other than the famous Adam Cain?"

Salwan frowned. "I would say you are mistaken. Adam Cain is old—for a Human—if he is even still alive. This Human is much younger."

"And that is where you are mistaken, Salwan. You see, I have access to information very few are privy to. I know for a fact that Adam Cain still lives, and with the help of the equally famous mutants Panur and Lila Bol, he was cloned to his present state. I do not know if this cloning has made him immortal, as are the mutants, but it would almost seem so from the feats he has accomplished. And now you send an overwhelming force against him, and they are all slaughtered, which only adds to the mystery."

"He cannot be immortal. He was injured as well in the bombing and only recently was released from the medical facility. Tenacious, but not immortal."

"That may be true, and it will be your task to find out for sure."

Salwan shook his head, confused. "Did you not tell me to do nothing?"

"You will do nothing—on the surface. Adam Cain will come for you, and when he does, you must be ready."

Salwan smiled, but it wasn't from humor. "That was my plan. But now you wish me to be a target?"

"Do you doubt your ability to plan an effective defense?" Davos asked.

"I do not. However, if what you say about this Human is correct, I would be putting myself in grave danger."

"You are already in grave danger. I have studied the extensive history of this Human. He seldom fails, if ever. That is why the trap you set for him must be failproof. Your life will depend on it."

"Why are you asking me to do this? Again, am I being punished simply for following your orders?"

Davos hesitated briefly before answering, locking his green orbs on Salwan's large, black eyes. "You seem to be confused, Salwan. I am not *asking* you to do this. I am telling you. Either face Adam Cain … or face me."

Salwan glanced around at the others in the room. He wished Davos had spoken to him like this in private, but the damage was already done. Besides, all of Salwan's entourage knew who was truly in charge. All Salwan had to do now was not to cower in the face of overwhelming authority.

"Of course, I will do as you command. That is why I control the Dravis Branch on your behalf. We will be ready for the Human's arrival, and at that time, you will find how inconsequential he truly is. One tiny Human cannot stand against the might of the Sylos Syndicate, no matter what his name is. And I will prove to you that Adam Cain is not any more immortal than you or me."

Davos grinned humorously. "I would expect nothing less."

11

The planet Ropor was only thirty-six hours away from Tel'oran, which was plenty of time for the bad guys to prepare for his arrival … if they would be waiting for him at all. Although Siri and he were attacked, there was still no way for Salwan's people to know for sure what the pair had learned. Everyone who had direct contact with them was dead. But if it were Adam, he would be figuring the worst. And now, the Human had left the planet. He could only be going to one place. The planet Ropor.

"Beth, what can you tell me about Salwan Saif and the planet Ropor?"

Adam could have just as easily referenced the Galactic Library himself, but Beth could do it much faster while simultaneously researching multiple avenues of inquiry, often things he would have never thought about.

"Salwan Saif is a business being of considerable wealth and influence, not only on the planet Roper but throughout much of the Darius Branch of the Orion Spur," the pleasant female voice of his ship's A.I. recited. "I have volumes of data relating to over two hundred business entities under his direction, with legal and financial documents. As you would assume, they appear to all be in order since he has had no probes by governmental entities beyond the normal nuisance cases."

"Almost too clean," Adam said.

"Precisely," Beth agreed. "That is why there is also extensive information about his purported criminal activities. Although hundreds of his subordinates have been found guilty of various crimes, Salwan Saif has never faced prosecution himself. That is standard for people of his status."

"What are some of these criminal activities he's suspected of being involved in?"

Adam was seated in the pilot seat of the *Arieel*, drinking a Diet Pepsi and staring idly out the front viewport at the computer-generated image outside. At his current speed—and traveling within the event horizon of millions of microscopic black holes—the area forward of the *Arieel* was only a single point of light, while all around the ship, there was utter darkness, as no light could catch up to the speeding starship. But Beth knew what space outside would look like to an outside observer, and she created a perfect representation of streaking stars and passing nebula in all the glorious colors of the universe. Mentally, an image like this was more comforting for sentient beings, so nearly all ships traveled in this mode.

"Salwan Saif's primary activities involve the theft and resale of fuel pods, operating a multi-world network of thieves, and creating an active marketplace for his merchandise. But that is only part of his operations. This list is three hundred fourteen items long, of which he has an interest. Do you wish to hear the list?"

"No, that's not necessary," Adam said. "And his headquarters is on Ropor?"

"It is, although, as expected, he has holdings on one hundred four other worlds. His primary operations are conducted out of a fortified compound sixteen kilometers west of the city of Ben'alin. He seldom goes into the city. There is a spaceport on his property."

"Can you show me an aerial view of his compound?"

"I can, although the interior beyond the outer walls is shielded from optical view. However, I believe I can take side-angle views from various sources to recreate the interior. It will take me a moment."

Three seconds later, a fairly detailed representation of Salwan's compound appeared on the forward viewscreen.

"Thank you, Beth. Now scan out; I need to see the lay of the land for twenty miles in all directions."

The scene changed, and Adam was able to switch between views and other slides with the use of his ATD. The two A.I. lovers were being very professional at the moment, obeying his directions without any superfluous flirting like they used to do. Adam grinned. Maybe now that they had a 'child,' a lot of the teenage spark had left the relationship, replaced now by a more mature acceptance of each other. Even so, Adam often felt a wave of joy sweep through his senses when he returned to the *Arieel* with Charlie. The A.I.s hated to be apart.

Now, Adam got down to business. He knew Salwan would be expecting him and would be watching every ship that landed at the commercial spaceport outside Ben'alin. Whether that would be where they'd attack him was in doubt. Would Salwan cause a scene until it was necessary? Besides, the gangster would want to know what Adam knew and who he and Siri had told. Adam smiled. He knew the bad guys would also be coming after Siri again, and that would be a major mistake. They wouldn't be getting any information from her, only the need for more bodybags.

So, if they could, they would try to take Adam alive. This contradicted their actions on Tel'oran when they thought they could shut down any spread of the information by killing the two Starfire agents before they had a chance to talk to anyone. But now, Adam was coming to Ropor. This told Salwan that information *had* been gleaned from the bombers. Finding out how damaging that information could be would be a priority, even more so than simply killing Adam.

Even though Salwan would be trying to capture him,

the Human wasn't going to give him a chance. He had no intention of being subtle. Adam wasn't here to make arrests or even to focus his anger on a single individual. All of Salwan's people were guilty in Adam's eyes. So, he would come to Ropor to kill, to exact revenge. And he wasn't ashamed to admit it.

But like any operation where people were expecting you, Adam had to do the unexpected. The bad guys would have the spaceport covered, as well as any other unauthorized landings in the area. The thing about a starship, it could drop down anywhere, and not just in official spaceports. So, Adam would do what they least expected. He would land at the spaceport for all to see. After that, things could get interesting.

Ropor was an average Prime world, with large oceans, ample land masses and a pair of balancing ice caps. It was early spring in the part of the planet where Ben'alin was located, and Adam planned his arrival right about dusk. The gravity quotient was .87 of Juirean Standard, which placed it at about sixty-five percent of Earth's gravity. Like always, Adam had made the thirty-six-hour trip at nearly double Earth's gravity aboard the *Arieel*. He'd been on Tel'oran for two weeks lying in a hospital bed, and he needed to reenergize his Human muscles for the coming campaign. He would have liked more time to get conditioned, but this would do.

Adam spent half a day laying out his gear and prepping his weapons. He would have only one backup flash weapon with him. All the rest would be kinetic weapons of Human manufacture. He also studied the photos of the compound until they were memorized. He also had Beth watching the local news broadcast for any movements Salwan might be making that would warrant interest from the press. After all, he was probably the wealthiest person on the planet. His movements would cause news.

But from what she could discern, Salwan was at his compound and even hosting a corporate retreat the next night. That was great. Get all the rats into one cage. Although Salwan ran dozens of legitimate businesses, for Adam, none of his employees were innocent, not like the majority of employees in the Starfire Building back on Tel'oran. What was good for the goose was good for the gander.

At the designated time, the *Arieel* entered the atmosphere and followed the tower's landing vector. The flight path took twenty-two minutes from orbit to landing, with a landing spot toward the rear of the spaceport and back in the shadows. Once the transponder on the *Arieel* was read and the origin of the ship revealed, Adam was sure the landing spot was selected for its remote location. The ship was also required to stay in a holding pattern for another ten minutes, ostensibly so another flight could clear out of the way. Adam knew it was so that troops could get stationed ahead of time.

Once on the surface, the landing jets quieted, and the smoke cleared. The light from the cockpit blazed out like a serpent's eye, but no movement was noticed inside.

The *Arieel* was quiet, and it remained that way for thirty minutes before someone got the courage to approach the vehicle. Six soldiers in two-by-two cover formation moved up to the starboard hatch. There was a code box on the hull, and a uniformed, yellow-skinned alien went to flip open the cover so an electronic code breaker could be attached. He didn't get that far before a high-voltage charge ripped through his body. He was flung back, his body smoldering where it landed.

The rest of the team backed away and resumed their cover, along with the other twenty members of the strike team. They called for instructions and were told to secure the location and not to let anyone off the ship. And if no one tries to leave? Remain on-site for as long as it takes.

And so they settled in as the night grew darker, watching the *Arieel*. They would be watching all night if that was how long it took.

The cool wind was whistling in Adam's ears as he dove through the atmosphere on artificial wings of reinforced composite. The glider was radar-proof and painted black to match Adam's outfit and would be invisible from the surface. With slight twists of his body, the Human guided his movements, watching his speed by occasionally aiming up to bleed off some of the descent before diving again for the surface. This reminded Adam of his HALO parachute jumps in the Navy—High Altitude/Low Opening. *Hooah!*

Adam wore an oxygen mask, although he was now below the threshold where one was needed. But when he bailed out the back of the *Arieel*, he was close to twenty-thousand feet up when he needed the mask. Now, he soared through the air, aiming for a low rise of hills about five klicks from Salwan's compound.

Charlie was connected to Beth aboard the *Arieel*, so Adam knew that the ship had landed and that a compliment of soldiers were standing guard over the vehicle. Although the force was sizeable, he didn't kid himself that that was all the alien-power Salwan had available to him. In fact, as he drew closer to the compound, Charlie was able to get an estimate of the energy weapons stored within the walls of the facility. Adam stopped listening when the count started at one thousand.

The compound itself was about a quarter-mile square with six primary structures inside twenty-foot-high walls. The main building was eight stories tall and dominated the estate. It looked more like an office building than a residence, and that was probably what it was. This was where Salwan ran his various enterprises. A three-building complex sat at the base of the larger building, forming a 'U' with a courtyard in the middle. This was probably where Salwan lived. Then, on the other side of the office structure, there was a pair of two-story buildings that looked to be barracks.

Charlie identified two main concentrations of weapons that were unmoving, meaning they were probably armories. That was where the bulk of the weapons were stored. But that still left plenty of wandering contacts to contend with. In fact, there were far more than one would expect on an average night on Ropor, even with a corporate retreat taking place. Everyone seemed to be armed, and that number ran into the hundreds. They were ready for Adam, even though outwardly, they tried to act like they weren't.

Adam had images of Salwan in Charlie's memory that could be used for facial recognition the moment the fighting began. Honestly, he didn't care if he had to kill every alien to get to the leader. He just didn't want to. But counting the flash weapon contacts and knowing how much ammunition and explosives he had with him, he had enough to do the job.

The ground swept up under him, and he pressed forward on the control bar, bringing the hang glider to a stop and dropping it to the surface. He had a little too much forward momentum, causing him to take several exaggerated steps before he finally tripped and fell face-first into the tall green grass. His oversized backpack rolled up on him, forcing him to eat even more grass before he came to a stop and untangled himself from the glider. He looked around nervously, embarrassed, hoping no one saw his awkward landing. That would never make it into his memoir. And if any of his SEAL buddies had been there, he would have never heard the last of it.

A residual light filled the air, both from the glow of a nearby nebula in the night sky as well as a low cloud cover that reflected the light from both the compound and the nearby city of Ben'alin. The city was large, with a couple of million residents, and with the technology of a Tier-1 society. Ropor had two moons, a major and a minor, but neither was visible at this hour.

Adam had two heavy packs to carry the five klicks to the compound. Fortunately, the gravity was fairly light on Ropor, so Adam could do it without too much effort. Still, he knew he had to get everything into position and then take a moment to let his cloning juice recharge his batteries. He would need all his strength for the assault.

And an assault it was going to be, which made Adam wonder if that was what Salwan was prepared for. How could he be? Adam was a single person. He wouldn't be foolish enough to launch a headlong attack on the compound by himself, would he? More than likely, the guards would be on the lookout for a stealth incursion, someone lurking in the shadows with a sniper rifle. Adam laughed. Were they in for a surprise.

Lifting each pack onto a different shoulder, Adam set off for the compound. He'd studied the topography, so he knew the best route, and his night vision contacts gave him a clear view through the shadows.

Even with the light gravity, Adam was huffing, puffing and covered in sweat by the time he'd traveled the five kilometers. He stationed himself in a gully about a hundred yards from the northeast corner of the complex, letting the packs fall to the ground with infinite relief. Then he fell back on the soft grass and let his rapid healing do its thing. He would recover ten times faster than even the best-conditioned Human, and then he'd be ready to go.

Light spilled over the tall whitewash walls, and clearly, half of the lights in the six-story office building were lit. The complex was alive with activity, as the 'retreat' sounded more like a party. After a few minutes, Adam began opening his packs.

The first thing he pulled out was half a dozen miniature drones, then he set them off into the sky under Charlie's control. Instantly, images began to be relayed to Adam's brain through the ATD and projected onto his vision. What he saw was encouraging.

The party was centered around the courtyard of what Adam assumed was the residence and then extended out into a large open area covered in soft grass and manicured walkways. The interior of the compound looked more like a park than a fortress. Until now, it never had to serve as a fortress. There were a hundred chairs along with a dozen long tables laid out on the grass, and aliens of all kinds were milling about, drinking, and chatting while servants set the tables for a lavish dinner. It all seemed so innocent until Charlie told Adam that all the guests were armed and that their movements were anything but random. They patrolled certain areas, following a prescribed routine.

And then, much to Adam's surprise, Salwan Saif appeared from inside the house. He began making his way through the crowd, heading for a table that formed the top of the 'T' across the others.

None of this made sense, Adam thought. Salwan knew the *Arieel* had landed, yet here he was, exposing himself and making it look as if he didn't have a care in the world. Adam snickered. It didn't take a genius to figure out the strategy. Salwan was making himself a target designed to draw Adam out. The alien would probably be protected by the best diffusion shields money could buy, and, upon closer examination, there would only be a couple of places where Adam could get a clear shot. And those would be covered by hidden assets.

I am doing my best, Adam, Charlie said in his mind, *but I will be unable to disarm all the energy weapons within the time allotted. At the pace I am working, I would need two hours and ten minutes, even starting with the active weapon and then moving to the armories.*

That's okay, Charlie. Just clear the northside for me. I see a path along the back of the office tower and through that small grove of trees. That should give me some cover. Get ready. We go in five.

Adam had his weapons laid out, as well as a tactical vest with molle webbing. A dozen magazines of nine-millimeter ammo were in the webbing, while a gear belt held a pair of SIG Sauer semi-automatics circa 2040. These were lightweight, with specialized sights and could hold 22-round magazines. Then, a back holster held an MK-88. Against soft-bodied aliens, the smaller caliber ammunition had more than enough stopping power. Across his back, Adam had a 308 Winchester rifle, along with a pair of Uzi submachine guns with 50-round boxes. He also carried a modern projection blade rated for two-thousand degrees and guaranteed to make mincemeat out of any aliens that got within range. He also had a variety of Ka-Bar knives because everyone needed their bling.

He had four grenades held in a metal case on his waist. There was a danger they could detonate if hit by a flash bolt, so Adam would keep them locked away until he needed them.

But the *pièce de résistance* of his weaponry was a GE 412-G rotating barrel minigun. For a century, weapons manufacturers had been trying to build a hand-held Gatling gun, and they finally succeeded with the 412. Of course, it took alien composite materials and fancy electronics to make it work. And even the barrels were composite, which is what made it possible. But still, the weapon weighed forty-one pounds. It was doable, but when lugging along a quad of five-hundred-round ammo belts, it was more than most normal people could carry for very long. That's why the weapon came with an attached tripod.

The good thing about Adam and this particular weapon is he would be wielding it on a planet with only sixty-five percent of Earth's gravity. That meant the weapon itself would only feel like twenty-seven pounds, and with the corresponding reduction in the weight of the ammo belts, as well. Adam already had the minigun fed with a belt, ready for action.

All he needed now was to get through the wall.

And for that, he had an RPG—a rocket-propelled grenade.

The first rocket was aimed to the south, about two hundred yards from Adam's position. The rocket streaked off and impacted the white wall a split second later, erupting into a plume of fiery yellow and white, shattering the block wall construction.

The sounds of fake partying beyond the wall ended, and professional commands were shouted. The drones showed a uniform and disciplined reaction to the explosion, which drew all eyes and movement to the south.

And that was when Adam demolished a section of the wall to the north with another RPG.

The Human was on the move, sprinting with overburdened Human strength toward the smoking cavity in the wall. Fortunately, as the battle progressed, he would shed weight, making him more agile. But for now, he needed to make an impact, and that was what the 412 was for.

Charlie had the flash weapons highlighted on Adam's vision, and the Human took aim, holding the minigun along his right thigh and lighting it off. The weapon zinged as Adam squeezed off with short bursts, only about twenty rounds at a time, and the hummingbird-like whine of the weapon was music to Adam's ears. He sent a spread of hot lead into the cloud from the explosion, aimed at the lighted spots on his HUD. Alien bodies were literally torn in half. Through the haze, Adam couldn't tell how many he'd killed, but he could guess when the dots signifying the energy weapons no longer moved. All the others were moving and in a hurry.

Adam sprinted into the compound and turned left, running along the back of the office building, letting off more quick bursts from the minigun. It was guaranteed the aliens had never heard or seen a weapon like this before, and after an initial show of courage and defiance, they soon changed their tune and sprinted away, looking for whatever cover they could find.

Adam appeared from the side of the office tower and set his sights on the huge gathering area where, moments before, a fake dinner was being set. A dozen of the 'guests' had tipped over one of the plastic tables and were hiding behind it. Adam sent a neat line of bullet holes along the entire length of the table, splitting it in two and killing everyone behind it.

Then Adam looked to his left, to where Salwan had last been seen by the drones. He was no longer there.

Adam was beginning to take incoming fire, but most of the shots were wild and off-target, fired before targeting computers could lock on. To his surprise, most of the bolts zipping through the air were Level-1s. He wondered if Salwan had researched what it took to kill a Human or if the aliens were just panicking.

Adam took a break to toss three smoke canisters into the clearing. They exploded in clouds of white, blinding cover, although Adam could still see the enemy through his HUD, tracking the movement of their flash weapons. Most of the incoming fire was at a distance since Charlie had disarmed those in the general vicinity.

He strung his last belt into the minigun and strafed the residence. That had to be where Salwan retreated to, and now Adam began making his way in that direction. He was hit twice in the back by Level-1 bolts, but his diffusion shield protected him. He had copper wires running down the back of his legs to his shoes, where short metal spikes would discharge the electricity into the ground. The system was working, although Adam could feel the intense heat building up. At some point, the wires would melt, and the diffusion shield would become only so much dead weight.

Adam also had a thin screen over his head, a one-shot shield against headshots. The wires were much thinner and would only take one Level-1 bolt or two Level-2s.

Within the first three minutes of the battle, the shield was gone.

Adam still had his general Human tenacity against flash bolts, even Level-1s. It was true that a single Level-1 bolt could kill a Human, but that usually had to be a head-shot straight on. And Adam had a little extra strength against energy bolts thanks to his cloning juice. Even so, it was becoming a little dicey.

"How we doing, Charlie?" Adam yelled aloud over the roar of battle.

All nearby weapons are neutralized, but there are still more coming from the right. It takes approximately two-point-five seconds to disarm each weapon once I have a lock on it. But the enemy soldiers are running, which makes it—

Adam felt a piercing hot pain in his right side. The impact of the Xan-fi flash bolt threw him sideways and to the ground as he gnashed his teeth, doing his best to will the pain away. He felt a surge of energy as his cloning juice gave him a little extra kick. He knew the injury had to be bad to hurt like it did, but he didn't have time to worry about that. He crawled over behind a ceramic planter with a towering palm-like tree sprouting from the center. More flash bolts splashed around him.

He spun the metal case around that held his grenades. The minigun was out of ammo, which, in a way, was a relief. He unbuckled the shoulder strap and let the whale of a weapon fall to the ground. This would now make him more mobile and quicker with his reactions. He removed two grenades and tossed them a hundred yards in the light gravity toward a horde of aliens rushing through the smoke in his direction. He could tell most of them didn't know where he was, but that didn't matter. They were part of a herd, and they were coming his way.

The grenades exploded, which surprised everyone. Body parts were cast in all directions as the ranks broke apart. The third grenade was aimed at the small cluster of aliens that formed the forward phalanx. It landed in the middle of the nine-person grouping. Only one survivor was seen attempting to crawl away after the explosion, but he didn't get too far, missing an arm and half a leg.

It was then that Adam noticed that the white dots signifying the active weapons were gone. Had he killed all the enemy? Even if that were so, their weapons would still register.

"Charlie? Are you there?" Adam suddenly noticed a dull void in his consciousness. He was too wrapped up in the pain of the bolt and the heat of the battle to notice at first, but it was definitely there. Correction: It wasn't there. There was no connection to Charlie.

Adam felt his side under his right arm pit. He winced in pain and withdrew a hand covered in blood. Firming his resolve, he felt again, groaning in agony as he felt for his ATD. The pencil-size device was still there, although only about half of it was still under his skin. The rest he could clearly feel with his fingertips.

"Shit!" he growled. There was another wave of aliens

coming from the west. Adam pulled one of his Uzis and lit off with several quick bursts. Soldiers fell while others moved for cover. The smoke was clearing, and the enemy had zeroed in on his location.

Adam popped another magazine into the Uzi and strafed the field again. He was too much in the open. He had to get inside the house.

Without the weight of the minigun and the diffusion shield, Adam felt as light as a feather, and it showed in the blazing speed he exhibited as he ran into the courtyard and toward the closest door to the building. Small fires had erupted from burning curtains, and this side of the home would soon be fully engulfed. But it was a large structure and more than likely with its share of safe rooms.

Adam's side burned, and every time his right sleeve brushed against the open wound, he felt a stabbing pain, even through his cloning. And now Charlie was out of order. That was a major complication. He was on his own against the remaining soldiers, plus he'd lost his contact with the *Arieel*. The ship was supposed to lift off and come get him at the conclusion of the raid. Now, he would have to find alternative transportation. If he lived long enough to need it.

Not only that, but Charlie also had facial recognition for Salwan Saif. Adam had studied the images ad nauseum, so there was still a good chance he could recognize the crime lord. But there were no guarantees.

Adam had little time to appreciate the beauty of the

home's interior as a torrent of flash bolts streaked through the open door and windows on this side of the courtyard. There were bodies on the floor, but no one was alive in this wing. With the Uzi still in his hand, he moved deeper into the home, heading for the wing that formed the connecting length of the U-shaped building.

Bolts suddenly came at him from a hallway in front of him. Adam slipped to his side and sent a line of bullets through the wall. The soft alien construction was no match for the 9mm parabellum rounds. Adam heard bodies fall to the floor on the other side of the barrier.

The Human sprinted around the corner and fired at three retreating aliens, hitting two of them. And then another bolt hit his back. Adam spun around and cut another soldier in two. At the next wing, Adam found a group of six soldiers barricaded in front of a paneled double door. They fired wildly at Adam, who fell back into a side room, spraying the hallway with rounds from the Uzi. Then, the weapon went dry.

Adam drew one of his two SIG Sauers. This was a more modern model that had an extended, 22-round magazine. He did a quick look-see. There were still six guards at the door. This was promising. Whatever was on the other side of the door was important.

The Human took a quick inventory. He had eight nine-millimeter magazines for the SIGs, as well as the Remington rifle and the MK. He pulled the energy weapon from the back holster only to find it had melted from one of the hits he'd taken to his back. He tossed the weapon aside.

In a way, weapons were the least of his worries. There were literally a couple of hundred of them lying around the compound, left there by dead or dying aliens. It was his physical condition that had him most worried. He was feeling groggy, and the pain was stronger than it should be. He wasn't used to this. The only explanation was he was more severely injured than he knew. And if that was the case, he could suddenly keel over without too much notice. He had to put an end to this battle soon.

Adam had one grenade left, and it was tailor-made for just this circumstance. He withdrew the knobby, green ball and pulled the pin with his teeth, not to be macho, but because his left arm wasn't much help at this point, more evidence of his unknown injuries. It was just a casual toss down the hallway, and a moment later, his ears were ringing from the massive explosion within the closed space.

With the SIG in his hand, he sprinted from his hiding space and to the now-missing double doorway into the unknown room beyond. A quick count showed eight aliens, all suffering from the effects of the blast, either cupping their bleeding ears or wobbling on weak knees and crossed eyes. Adam paraded through the room, heading for the solitary figure on the other side. As he went, he Mozambiqued everyone he saw, living or dead.

Adam reloaded and continued to shoot until he was at

the far side of the room and standing before a cowering figure huddled behind a torn and blood-soaked couch. He tried to kick the couch aside but found the piece of furniture was more resistant than he expected. He recoiled back and fell to the floor, a strange tingling in his legs and hips.

The figure behind the couch rose up when he saw Adam fall. He had a weapon in his hand. He aimed it at the Human, a look of glee on his narrow alien face.

"You must be Adam Cain," said Salwan Saif. "No! Stop! He is mine," said the crime boss as five more soldiers rushed into the room. Adam glanced over at them. There were only five, and no backup came in after them. There would be no reason for others to wait outside. If there were more, they'd be here.

So, it's down to these six, Adam thought.

The injured Human pushed himself across the floor until his back met an overturned chair. He leaned against it and let out a long, loud breath, closing his eyes momentarily.

"Do not pass out on me, Human," Salwan said, stepping closer. "I am just starting with you."

Adam let his eyes flutter open, biding his time as his cloning juice worked overtime to get him back into even marginal operating condition. He didn't know if it would happen, but every second would help.

"Why," Adam moaned. "Why did you bomb the building? What did Starfire ever do to you?" Get him talking, boasting. Most criminal bigwigs had an ego to match their sadism. They loved to brag. But what Salwan said surprised him.

"Why, you ask? Because I was told to."

Adam raised his eyebrows; even that hurt.

"Does that surprise you, Human? Yes, even I have someone I answer to. But that matters not. I just want you to know that not only have you failed to kill me, but you have not even come close to exacting your revenge on the person ultimately responsible for the death of your friends and co-workers. You have sacrificed your life ... for nothing. Less than nothing."

Adam could feel the pain numbing and his muddled thoughts becoming clearer. But this was different. His recovery was being fought by a force every bit its equal; however, if there was one thing that gave Adam the will to survive, it was knowing that Salwan was not alone in the responsibility for killing his friends. He had to find out who it was and then live long enough to do something about it.

Unfortunately, Salwan wasn't going to give him the time to do it.

He lifted the weapon, aiming the flash weapon at his head. A Level-1, at this range and in that location, would be lethal.

And that's when Adam fired the SIG from his hip, hitting Salwan in the chest and throwing him back over the bloody couch. Adam then rolled onto his left side, raising the SIG Sauer in his right hand. The five alien soldiers were clustered near the door, with only about six feet separating them. Adam fingered the handgun with such speed and precision that it was hard to tell the shots apart. This was something the aliens had never witnessed before. Unfortunately for them, it would be the last thing they witnessed. Adam killed four of them outright, with the fifth taking a hit to the shoulder. Ripping wounds from kinetic weapons were generally unknown to aliens, so he was ill-prepared for the pain and agony that swept over him. He fell to the floor, shocked by the bloody mass of torn skin that had been his shoulder. The hollow point did its job, and if Adam didn't put the poor creature out of his misery, he would soon die of shock.

Adam grinned wickedly and let his weapon fall to the floor. And then, just like the wounded alien, Adam slumped over and passed out.

12

Adam heard chiming, like crystal dancing on crystal. It was a pleasant sound, musical and soothing. There was also the fresh scent of cut flowers swirling past his nose as a breeze, smelling of the outdoors, wafted past him.

The problem: He didn't know where any of this was coming from.

It was night, as far as he could tell. Everything was as black as black could be. Blacker than any night he knew of. Then he heard another sound, the sound of breathing. He tensed as the smell of perfume became even stronger.

Then the sun came up.

Or, more precisely, it enveloped him.

A black-lined shroud was lifted away from his head. Now, he squinted against the hard yellow light with flashes of reflections from a crystal windchime sparkling against chiffon curtains.

He was on a bed, or in this case, inside one. The mattress was one of the softest things he'd ever felt, making it seem as if he was floating in air, and the blankets and sheets were as light as feathers and smelled like a cool Spring day. Clearly, he was in Heaven, especially when he saw the female standing next to him. She was tall and exquisitely slender, with each curve of her body flowing into the next. Everything was smooth and symmetrical, and her near-see-through gown shimmered with an ephemeral glow like everything else in the room. She was not Human, which was the only thing that made him question the Heaven hypothesis. Her huge black orbs were long and narrow, her nose impossibly small, and the mouth wide and sensuous.

"How are you feeling this morning?" a sing-song voice filtered throughout the room. For a moment, Adam couldn't tell if it came from the vision standing before him or from somewhere else. Then she spoke again. "It appears you will not need the meditation dome anymore unless you specifically request it. I love using one when I am having trouble sleeping."

Adam was stunned into silence. This wasn't Heaven, but it was the next best thing.

Now, he looked beyond the bed, through a paneled window, to a brilliant garden of purple, red and yellow flowers. Birds chirped, and a breeze rustled the gossamer curtains.

"Where am I," Adam ventured to ask, almost afraid of the answer. It would be his luck that he'd be back in the Milky Way and just on some alien world with nothing having changed from the last memories he had.

And the memories were horrible.

It all came flooding back to him: the battle on the planet Roper, the white smoke, the sounds of battle, the bodies being blown apart, and then his killing of Salwan Saif. Then he remembered Charlie.

Adam twisted in the bed and ran his left hand over his right side under his armpit. The skin was rough and tender, and when he pulled his hand away, there was a sheen of sticky liquid on his fingers.

The slender goddess was looking at him with an amused look on her stunning face.

"You are being cared for by the graces of the *Charlema* Galena Gar. You are on the planet Dizona and in the Charlema's private residence. I am O'Palma, a medical attendant, part of your recovery team. You have been here for six of our days."

Adam quickly worked through his shock. "Thank you, O'Palma. That was very helpful. Is it possible for me to speak with Galena—the Charlema?"

The goddess smiled. "*Charlema* is a title of respect among my people. It translates into *The Mother of Generosity*. Galena has given much to my world."

Adam looked out the window again. "You have a lovely world. I've never heard of Dizona before."

"The Charlema keeps it private for her and her closest friends. You are privileged to be here. She rarely has visitors. Now, relax. I will go to her now. She has been anxious to speak with you."

As Adam waited, he tried to recall the last few minutes of his time on Roper, trying to figure out how he ended up here and in the care of the richest person in the galaxy. Adam had only met Galena Gar once, and that was a couple of years ago. Since then, he'd occasionally heard of her—when she scooped up a new major company that had fallen on hard times or when she bought another planet. She collected planets like some people collect vintage cars. Dizona had to be one of her gems if it lived up to the promise of the view he could see out the window. He was sure it did.

There was a rustling down the hall, and Galena swept into the room with O'Palma at her elbow. The lithe young creature carried a tray with a flask of caramel-colored liquid in it and two fluted glasses.

As it was the first time Adam saw the stunning alien mogul, he was taken aback by the smooth purple skin, high cheekbones and glowing golden eyes. But unlike the first time, Galena wasn't wearing an elaborate headdress of gold. Instead, her long, dirty blond hair was tied behind her head in a very standard—yet flattering—ponytail. But even if she wasn't flamboyant, she made up for it with the dress she wore. It was a kimono-like silk outfit colored in red and yellow swirls with a high collar, and it fit every sensual curve of her body to perfection. Between Galena and O'Palma, Adam was experiencing stimulation overload.

"My friend, Adam Cain," Galena greeted with a smile that would put a supernova to shame. "I am so pleased that you are feeling better. For a while, my doctors were not encouraging. But I assured them that you have powers of healing that would amaze them. And you have."

"Thank you," Adam muttered. "But, why … how did I get here?"

Galena swung a shapely hip at the side of the bed and sat down next to Adam. "I will tell you, but first, a refreshment. O'Palma…"

The native had placed the tray on a side table; now she filled two glasses with a thick, yellowish liquid looking almost like honey. Even from a distance, Adam caught the scent of jasmine.

O'Palma passed the glasses to Galena and Adam, and then she bowed gracefully and left the room.

"She is a charming person," Galena observed, "as are all the natives. In my opinion, they are the best-kept secret in the galaxy."

"Because *you* keep it a secret," Adam said with a smile.

"I have a lot of secrets." Galena lifted her glass; Adam mirrored her. "I believe this a tradition on your world. You call it a toast, of which I will be forever confused. The Human language is so complex, with layers of contradictions. But the Humans seemed to deal with it without complaint."

"It's our language," Adam said, even though Galena knew only a fraction of it. Even today, after fifty years of alien interaction, there are still hundreds of languages spoken on Earth. That was unusual in the galaxy, where most worlds had one dominant language.

"To your rapid recovery and a taming of your angry soul."

Adam frowned slightly, not understanding the second part of the toast. He was sure Galena would get around to explaining herself. Adam sniffed the liquid, feeling a head rush from the sweetness of it.

"It has already been tested for safety," Galena reported.

Adam took a sip.

He didn't know how much time passed before he became aware of the room again. In reality, it was only a couple of seconds. The sweetness lingered, literally bringing Adam to tears with the power of the intoxicating taste. He took a second sip. It was every bit as startling as the first.

"It is called *flasia* and is made from the mixing of two of the most fragrant flowers on Dizona, along with the nectar from a native insect. And on a planet of fragrance, that is saying something. And I should tell you, each glass has an estimated value of two hundred seventy-five *thousand* energy credits. It is in the Galactic Library as the most expensive drink in existence."

Galena took her glass and downed it in three large swallows. "I cannot get enough of this stuff."

Adam's mouth hung open as Galena twisted around and poured herself another glass. The flask had to hold a couple of million ECs worth of liquid gold, although gold wouldn't even come close to the value of this drink.

Hey, this is on Galena's dime, so what the hell. Adam finished off his glass and then held it out for a refill, wearing a silly grin on his face.

Galena laughed wholeheartedly and filled the glass.

"It is also slightly intoxicating, although very few ever notice. You must drink a lot to feel the effects."

"And you have?" Adam asked wickedly.

"All the time."

Adam was on his third glass of *flasia* when he got down to business.

"Okay, Galena, what's going on? Why am I here, and how are you involved?"

The purple-skinned alien sat her glass down on the tray and then twisted on the bed so she could look at Adam full-on. "It is quite simple. I heard of the tragedy on

Tel'oran and immediately grew concerned for you. Although we hardly know each other, I was in your debt for what you did on Tactori regarding the dark energy generator."

Adam smirked. "I'm also sure you were a little pissed when the planet didn't blow up, leaving you running all the finances in the galaxy."

Galena smiled, her eyes sparkling. "Not all opportunities materialize. However, I still profited from the emergence of the Affiliation of Planets, which would never have happened if Tactori had been destroyed. Continuing: I researched to find out if you were among the dead and was relieved to find you were not. I further investigated whether or not you were in continuing danger after the attack and concluded that you were. That is when I began to actively follow your actions."

"You've been spying on me?"

"I spy on everyone to one degree or another. It is how I gain information, and information leads to opportunity. Now, let me finish. I tracked you to Ropor, and my people observed the battle that took place. We found your body only moments before you would have expired. You were frozen and brought here, where you have been under my care ever since."

Adam felt his right side again. "My ATD—my Artificial Telepathy Device. You knew about it before."

"Yes. Apparently, you took a direct hit on your right

side, and the device was overloaded. I have enlisted the services of two Formilian technicians who have been working diligently to restore functionality. It is still a work in progress."

"Again, why are you doing this ... for me?"

"You forget, Adam Cain, I know all about you. I know the miracle that took place that allows you to be here and in the form I see before me. At one time, I mentioned my desire to learn your secrets. I know they are not of your own doing, that you were merely a recipient of the genius offered by Panur and Lila. But I still desire that knowledge." Galena grinned sweetly again. "And if there is one thing to know about me, I usually get what I want."

"Have you? Gotten what you wanted, I mean?"

"That, too, is a work in progress. My doctors have had an opportunity to study you while you have been convalescing. We have all we need to continue the research, but so far, there have been no major breakthroughs. But it is still early."

"And here I thought it might be because you liked me."

Galena pursed her lips and looked Adam directly in the eye. "I believe you already know the answer to that."

Now that Adam had asked the question, he wasn't quite ready for her direct answer. He felt his face burn from embarrassment. He quickly changed the subject.

"You know, you could have just asked for my help with your medical tests. They're doing the same thing back on

Tel'oran, hoping to find something that will help Tidus. Tidus is my boss."

"I know of the Juirean. As I said, I have been studying you. But be it as it may, we have both benefited from my fortuitous intervention. You have been nursed back to health, and I have the raw materials that may lead to my immortality."

"You know I'm not immortal."

"Of course I do. And I also know that cloning is a fairly routine procedure. But you are unique in that you were cloned with all your memories and personality intact. That has never been done before."

Adam shook his head. "I have to tell you, that was all Panur's doing. It wasn't part of the cloning. He has the ability to absorb people's memories and then transplant them into other bodies. If he hadn't done that with me, I would have come out of the cloning like a newborn baby, having to learn everything all over again."

"I realize that. And that is a problem for another time. But at the moment, I would settle for an elixir that could reverse the aging process, or at least slow it down, as it has in your case."

Galena's face turned serious. "This may be a road to nowhere, but I am in the unique position of being able to pursue even my wildest fantasies. I am also a creature of opportunity, and when the opportunity came to study you in more depth, I took it."

Adam smirked. "Hey, I'm not complaining. I think it

was a fair trade. I just don't want you to get your hopes up."

"Do you know where the mutants are?" Galena asked. It was a common question for anyone who knew who Adam really was.

"I'm afraid not. At one time, I thought they were always watching over me and would show up when I really needed them." He shrugged. "Hell, Salwan's compound would have been a nice place for that to happen. I'm just glad someone did. And thanks for that."

"My pleasure."

Adam looked around the exquisitely decorated room—charming, if a little frilly for his tastes. "So, what happens now?"

"You must still recover, although that stage should be complete in a day or so. The Formilians still have processes to go through with your interface device." She turned serious. "And you will have to resolve your lingering issues."

Adam smirked. "And what issues would those be?"

"I sense you do not feel your mission is complete, your revenge satisfied."

Adam shook his head. "Salwan said he was acting on orders. I need to find out who pulls his strings."

Galena frowned as she worked through the translation. "I understand. But I need to warn you. There are forces at work of which you have very little understanding. You may not like what you find."

Adam felt the hair stand up on the back of his neck. If anyone had the answers to his questions, it would be the purple-skinned beauty. She ran the galaxy, and if he was smart, he would heed her warning.

But that wasn't how Adam Cain rolled.

13

"Perhaps you should tell me what you know."

Adam was afraid the path might lead back to her. And if that were the case, he wasn't sure what he would do.

Galena poured herself another glass of *flasia* and then pursed her lips. The flirtatious and lighthearted Galena Gar was gone, replaced with the pragmatic, serious galactic power broker.

"Adam, there are layers of authority throughout the galaxy as well as on every planet and within every society. Some are major, some are minor, but it is the nature of civilization. These layers are made up of familial, private, corporate and governmental entities. I happen to occupy the uppermost level of authority, along with a relative few of my status. We call ourselves *The Community*. This is not bragging; this is being realistic.

"Within my caste, policies are established that others on the levels below us are tasked with implementing. Most of the time, we have no idea what steps are being taken to implement these policies, and in all honesty, we do not want to know. As you can imagine, these methods often cross the line between legal and illegal activities. But because those of us on my level have had no input into these methods or means—and are so far removed—we are held apart, immune from the circumstances. And our decisions cover every imaginable activity taking place across the galaxy.

"However, it should also be known that few criminal enterprises—and none of any significance—can exist without at least the tacit approval from people like me. It is the nature of existence. We control everything. So, you see, everyone has someone else to answer to ... unless you are at my level.

"Furthermore, for large systems to operate, such as a galaxy, laws *must* be broken, rewritten or circumvented. That is unavoidable. Nothing can function when chained to artificial and shortsighted restrictions and often written by people who have no clue what is really going on. And who do you think makes the decisions as to what to change and what to stay the same? *The Community*."

"I don't care anything about that," Adam said passionately. "I'm not naive. I know that the so-called elites run the show. Money and power go hand-in-hand. And no one has more money than you do. I'm not trying to change anything. I'm not on some noble quest of good over evil, right over wrong. All I want is justice for what someone—somewhere—did to me and my friends. This is personal."

Galena was quiet for a moment, lost in thought. Then, she refocused her attention on Adam. "Then, I, too, will make it personal," she announced. "But only within limits." Adam waited for her to continue. "You wish to know who is ultimately responsible for what happened on Tel'oran? I will tell you. And once I have, I will tell you why. It is Davos Pannel. Perhaps you already suspected as much."

Adam's mouth fell open. "Why would I suspect him? I don't even know who—wait, I've heard that name before."

"You should have … you killed his brother."

"*Daxian* Pannel!" Adam exclaimed. "That's right. But I didn't kill him. I was trying to save him when he died."

"That seems immaterial at the moment, does it not? The Pannel brother is dead, and Davos ordered the bombing of the Starfire Building."

Adam pushed up on the bed, sitting up straighter, anger swelling inside him. "If you knew he was going to do that, why didn't you tell me?"

Galena recoiled, furrowing her brow. "I did not know beforehand. I only learned afterward. And even that was fortuitous. We were at an event together recently and he spoke briefly of it."

"He told you! What did you say to him?"

"Do not bark at me like that! I am not one you can

treat in such a manner. Besides, I am your friend ... if you will allow me."

Adam calmed down ... a little. "I'm sorry. But I still want to know what you said to him when he told you he bombed the Starfire Building."

"I said nothing," Galena said sternly.

"Nothing?"

"Nothing, and I will tell you why if you stop yelling at me."

Adam held up his hands in mock surrender.

Galena gathered herself before continuing. "As I said, those of us on my level seldom—never—are involved in the actual operations that result from our directives. It is an unspoken rule, not only for the individual's good but for the good of The Community."

"Yeah, we call it *plausible deniability*."

"Precisely. But when Davos took personal control, he crossed that sacred barrier between legal and illegal, between our people and everyone else.

"You may not see this as a real barrier, but to us, it is. What happens to one could potentially bleed over to the rest of us. Not only that but because of this barrier, I can sleep at night, even though there may be horrific things being done in my name. If there was no barrier, then even I would become subject to the verities of doubt and conscience. I hope this makes sense to you, Adam. But when one of us takes a personal hand in an illegal act, especially one as horrific as mass murder, then he forfeits his immunity for the good of all of us."

"And that's what he did; he took an active role?"

"He did. Even though he may have felt he was justified after the death of his brother, there were other ways to go about it. But his need for revenge caused him to break the rules. And one should never do that."

"What happens when someone does that—when they break the rules?"

Galena gave Adam a sinister smile. "On Earth, you would say they are thrown to the wolves, meaning they must be excised from The Community before they infect us all. That is why I told you of Davos' complicity. If there is a major investigation that leads back to him, it could tarnish us all."

Adam snorted. "So, you want me to do your dirty work for you?"

"I understand the meaning … and I suppose I do. However, it is a consequence of what you were already planning to do."

"Well, not really, not until you told me it was Davos."

"I did that for a reason. Davos has been actively looking for you since the battle on Ropor. He suspects you are alive, and if you killed Salwan, he must assume you learned who instructed him to destroy Starfire. If you are not actively looking for him—or on guard—then he could easily eliminate you before you know who is targeting you.

I do not want that to happen. So, to even the odds, Davos Pannel is fair game."

Adam smirked. "And if he goes down, then many of his operations become fair game as well ... for the corporate vultures."

"Like me?" Galena asked her expression even.

"Like you," Adam confirmed.

"I make no apologies. I am a seeker of opportunity, that is all. In a way, every living creature is that way. It is required for survival. However, in my case, I have the means to act more quickly and decisively and on a much grander scale when opportunities arise. And chaos—in its many varieties—breeds opportunity. Chaos, Adam Cain, is my playground."

Adam nodded knowingly. "Mine, too, but more as a creator than an opportunist. I wish you well when the next upheaval happens, Galena. I believe you know when that might be happening."

"I do," Galena said, her forehead furrowing. "And although I thrive on chaos, I still wish no harm to come to you. I would forgo this coming opportunity if it would guarantee your safety. But I am a realist. I know that neither you nor Davos will rest until one of you is dead. If I could do more to give you an advantage, I would."

Adam tapped the side of his torso under his right arm. "Helping get Charlie working again will be a great help."

"I understand the device is still configuring. Again, if

there is anything I can do short of taking an active role in negating Davos, just ask."

Adam reached out and took Galena's hand. It was the first time they had touched, and it was electric. "I appreciate that," he said. "Would it be permissible to get me information on Davos and his operation, where he lives, who's protecting him, things like that?"

"I can do that since that information is readily accessible from other sources. Believe me, Adam. I must be careful. As I said, everyone on every level answers to someone else. And I answer to my contemporaries—who shall remain anonymous." She grinned sorrowfully. "Now, get more rest. The Formilians will be in later to continue working on your device—your Charlie device."

Adam pulled her back by the hand as she went to leave. "Oh, and where's my ship?"

Galena smiled warmly at him before leaning over and giving him a full kiss on the lips. That was unexpected—and heavenly.

"I brought it to Dizona."

Adam frowned. "How did you do that? My A.I. has specific orders that no one is to disturb the ship."

"You mean Beth? She was delightful and fully cooperative once she realized I was there to help you. I had my people take very good care of her—the *Arieel*, is that right?"

Adam nodded.

"I know an Arieel ... from Formil. Arieel Bol, the Speaker. She is such a sweet person. Do you know her?"

Adam swallowed hard. "Yeah, we've met."

Galena met his eyes with a twinkle. "That is interesting. I would like to hear the stories." And then she left, leaving Adam wondering just how much the Queen of the Milky Way knew about him and Arieel ... and Lila. This could get complicated.

14

True to her word, Adam got access to reams of information on Davos Pannel and his operations. Adam had heard a little about the Sylos Syndicate throughout the years, but he didn't know the full extent of their operations. For Davos to move in Galena's circles meant he had to be either fabulously wealthy or immensely powerful. He was both.

In fact, Adam was sure no one other than Galena and her crowd knew the full extent of the Syndicate's operations; hell, they probably didn't know themselves. They were that big. It was like Adam asking Galena how many planets she owned. At first, she said nine, but then she backtracked, saying eight. Then she counted again. It was eleven. Eleven whole planets. Of course, as Galena explained, they weren't all populated worlds. Some she owned simply for the natural resources they could provide.

Others were inhabited by smaller populations, and she was more like a governor to them than an overlord. And then there was Dizona.

After Adam was fully healed, he and Galena took several long tours of the garden planet. The place was a paradise, with a stable population of about half a billion of some of the most gorgeous Primes Adam had ever seen. Where the Formilians were stunning because of their extreme feminine and masculine perfection, the Dizonaeans were simply angel-like in their appearance and manners. They were so incredibly gentle and peaceful that Adam begged Galena to make sure the word never got out about the planet. It would be fair game for the seedier side of the galaxy's population, and any outside influences would be sure to destroy the native's fragile existence. Galena assured him that was her plan. Dizona was her little treasure, and she was going to keep it that way.

Adam was at a desk in his luxurious apartment suite Galena had provided for him, going over images of the planet Racitor, where Davos spent most of his time. The data Galena's people provided was some of the best intelligence he'd ever seen. They gave him personnel strength numbers, bios, and troop concentrations, along with all the addresses and images—both satellite and interior—of nearly all his site locations. It was a lot of information, but Adam was concentrating on Racitor.

Not that he wanted to. He would have preferred to take the crime lord on one of his lesser holdings and not surrounded by the strength of his organization. But a person's headquarters is where they're most comfortable, the place where they let down their guard. Besides, Adam hadn't yet decided how extensive he wanted to make his mission. Did he want to just take out Davos? Or did he want to bring down the whole operation?

That last one seemed almost impossible, and he wasn't sure if there would be repercussions for Galena's associates if he did. When he brought up the subject, Galena laughed. First, there was the idea that one person could bring down the Syndicate, and second, Adam would temper his operation to protect her. She assured him that whatever chaos he could create would benefit her in spades. As she said, she was a creature of chaos. If she was given lemons, she would make a fortune by cornering the market for lemonade throughout the galaxy.

Galena came into the room and placed two soft hands on his shoulders. The pair had consummated their burgeoning relationship two nights before, and Adam was still walking on air recalling the memory. Even though it had been heavenly and with abandon, Adam still felt Galena was holding back. It may have been a defense mechanism on her part since being the richest person in the galaxy made her the target of many an unscrupulous plot to take some of her wealth from her, some of which involved affairs of the heart. Adam accepted that. Besides, he wasn't ready for much more himself. Hell, he wasn't even sure he'd be alive in a couple of weeks, let alone long enough for the pair to bond to any significant level. For the moment, it was primarily physical, which satisfied the two lovers to the point of childlike giddiness.

Adam had been looking at a map of the planet Racitor and plotting out all of Davos' various holdings. The map looked as if it had a severe case of measles. But one spot seemed out of place. He asked Galena about it.

She leaned over and looked at the point that was seemingly in the middle of a vast ocean sea, much like the Gulf of Mexico on Earth.

"Is that an island?" he asked her.

"Not a natural island," she replied. "It is the site of his underwater habitat. It is an extensive structure sitting at a reasonable depth within a reef of wonderous colors and teeming life. It is his pride and joy. He spends much of his time there when he is on Racitor."

"Have you been there?"

"No, I have not. Perhaps one day—" Then she caught herself. "You know what I meant."

Adam patted her hand. "I do. Now, this is interesting." He studied the map more as an idea came to his mind. "You say he spends a lot of time there?"

"Yes. What are you thinking about? The structure is under the sea."

Adam chuckled. "I know. Isn't that great!"

Galena was lost in his enthusiasm. "If I gave you a list of items, could you get them for me?" he asked.

Galena frowned. "That depends. And if I can, it will be done by others, and you will have to pay for everything. I cannot have any such purchases traceable to me."

"I'm okay with that. Let me get the list—"

Adam Cain.

The voice rang out in his mind. Adam jumped at the interruption, only realizing now how much he'd missed the thick presence that had been Charlie—his ATD.

"Excuse me, Galena. I have to take this call."

The purple mogul shook her head in confusion as Adam retreated into himself, silent but his face animated. It only took her a moment to realize what he was doing.

Charlie! I am so glad to hear from you. How are you feeling?

The question is nonsensical, came the mental reply. *I am incapable of having feelings.*

Dammit, Adam thought on another level unknown to his ATD. He was afraid of this. When the Formilian techs rebooted him, it was possible he would resort back to his basic programming, losing all the years of interaction—and growth—Adam had seen from the A.I. He hoped it would only be temporary.

You know what I meant, Adam thought to his ATD. *Are you back to full function?*

I am still running through my programming. It could take a while before I have a full assessment. But as far as the interface, that is fully functional. I am available for requests.

Good. Standby. I'm working on a plan that's going to require some of your input.

I await your orders.

Adam broke the mental link and looked back at Galena. She was still standing over him, her eyes clouded.

"Charlie is back," he told her. "But he's not quite himself."

"What do you mean?"

"He's rather basic. I'm hoping he'll get his personality back. He was like having a teammate and friend on every mission. It was a lot of fun, and I never felt alone."

Galena laughed. "That is amazing. I must get myself one of those."

Adam was about to say, *'Yeah, good luck with that. The Formilians guard their 'Gifts' like Earth used to guard Ft. Knox.'* Then he remembered who he was talking with. Hell, she'd probably have her own ATD by sunset.

He shuddered to think what Galena Gar could do if she had an ATD.

"If you will excuse me now," Adam said politely, "I have some planning to do."

She kissed him on the cheek and left him to his thoughts. He was excited. This would be something familiar … yet different. After all these years, he wondered if he still had the skills to pull it off.

. . .

Adam had not wanted to commit to a mission until Charlie was back online. Now that he was—even a rudimentary Charlie—he pushed ahead with electric enthusiasm. He made up a list of what he might need for the mission and then passed it along to Galena. She didn't look at the datapad; instead, she passed it to a Dizonaean, who took it without question or instructions. Three days later, Adam received a bill for three million energy credits. He gagged a little but helped the native link to his bank account on Tel'oran. Once the transfer was made, he was told the items would be aboard the *Arieel* in two weeks. Even galactic elites had to deal with the time delay in moving products from one part of the galaxy to the next. Still, this was faster than anyone else could have rounded up the gear.

In the meantime, Adam received rudimentary schematics for the underwater facility, which Davos called *Varosia*, but only for the exterior. The interior layout was restricted. Even so, Adam could tell it was a pretty fancy operation, designed for living rather than research, as were most of the similar facilities on Earth. It was made up of nearly all windows with incredible views of the underwater world. It began at a depth of only twenty meters, with the deepest part at fifty meters. In the crystal-clear waters of the tropical sea, this afforded ample light to view the seascape, although three hundred strategically placed floodlights also did the job around the clock. That could be an issue—too much light. But Adam would deal with that if he had to.

He only had a germ of a plan at the time, but each hour, each day, he gained detail. The number one issue was making sure Davos would be there. This required a little more research into the movements of the Syndicate leader. The fact that Davos still believed Adam was alive could work to his advantage, and the more time that passed would make the mogul even more paranoid. He knew an attack was coming; Adam's background left no doubt about that. When and where was the question? And because of that, Adam noted that Davos' movements were becoming more restrictive. He only visited a handful of his operations on Racitor, and he made more frequent visits to Varosia. The underwater retreat was his go-to place, a location where he felt the most secure since it was so little known and off the beaten path. No official business was conducted there, so very few people knew of its existence. And it was also underwater.

Charlie was helping out, electronically connecting with Galena's vast array of the most advanced computers in the galaxy. It reminded Adam of the time he used the Klin computers aboard a derelict Colony Ship. Although the system was old, it was still the best computer system in the galaxy. The Klin knew their stuff when it came to technology. Adam shrugged. They should; the Aris taught them everything they knew. But that was another story.

Galena's system allowed Adam to track Davos' movements as if he were on Racitor itself. It also allowed the Human to spread some of his savings around, remotely hiring native Racitoreans for various jobs, splitting tasks among a dozen entities so neither one saw the whole picture. When Adam got to the planet, he would bring everything together.

And that time was coming near. Charlie was functional, if not the trusty side-kick Adam once had. But he was coming along … slowly. Adam rarely connected Charlie to Beth inside the *Arieel*, although his ship's A.I. spoke of him often. She knew his present state of mind, so no one mentioned Davy—their joint and still-developing computer program. Neither Adam nor Beth wanted to shock him with the news until they felt he was ready, or he brought up the subject himself. The fact that he hadn't made any such overture made them suspect that part of his memory may be lost forever. That would have been a shame. Adam also wondered why Charlie didn't have a backup somewhere to recover fully in the event of something like this happening, and both Adam and Charlie knew it was more of a when rather than if. Adam decided to talk to Beth about this when he was back on the Arieel—a backup for both Charlie and her.

Adam finally decided on a departure date. It would take another three long weeks to reach Racitor, and Adam could put the final touches to his plan on the way there. What Adam regretted was leaving Galena. He'd been on Dizona for two months and had fallen under its spell.

Sharing a bed with Galena was a big part of that. Neither of them had ventured much beyond the physical, with no talk of the future. Adam was about to embark on the most dangerous mission of his life, so it didn't make sense to think much beyond that.

Which raised another question: Why was Adam still so dead set on going after Davos?

He'd made a couple of calls to Siri—where he promptly got his ass chewed for not keeping her up-to-date more often. She told him that Tidus was responding to the new treatments the doctors had devised for him and was out of the coma. In fact, he was making remarkable progress. That was a relief to Adam, but it did remind him of why he was on Dizona in the first place. If the trail had ended with Salwan, he would have gladly turned in his badge and thought about settling down. But seeing that the job wasn't over yet, he firmed his resolve to complete it. And if only Davos died, then that would be enough. Once he learned the connection between the death of Daxian and Davos, he saw that what happened to Starfire was more a direct result of Adam's actions than a sinister conspiracy against the company by an evil conglomerate. It was personal, not business.

That simplified the mission. All Adam had to do was take out Davos and he could call things even. Then he grimaced. That wasn't quite right. Nothing could square the ledger on all the people who died in the bombing. But killing a bunch of strangers wouldn't bring any of them back. And after talking to Siri, Adam felt an overpowering desire to go home again … home to Tel'oran.

Even so, the farewells were teary, causing Adam to give a quick nod to Galena and O'Palma before ducking into the *Arieel* and slamming shut the pressure door before he lost it completely. Even after returning to space, Adam was a basket case for a while, wondering what in the world was happening to him. Here he was, getting all sentimental about friends and lovers. But that wasn't the strange part. What was frankly unbelievable was that they were all *aliens*. What had happened to Adam Cain, the alien with an attitude? He was a notorious alien-hater, and now there were aliens who actually cared for him … and he cared for them. At least some of them he did. But it was a start. Adam gnashed his teeth in frustration. *It certainly took you long enough, dickhead!*

15

During the trip to Racitor, Adam worked diligently in the cargo hold, building the devices he needed. Galena had come through with the necessary ingredients, some of which he was sure required permits and licenses to acquire. She had gotten everything in a couple of weeks.

His plan was twofold.

First, drive Davos from his shore residences and to his underwater refuge. Then, second, gain entry to Varisa and take out the bad guy.

Exfil could be an issue, depending on how bloody things get in the habitat. But the *Arieel* would be on standby, ready to sweep in and rescue him if the need arose.

. . .

It was the same old hurry up and wait that always annoyed Adam about space travel. He'd left Dizona raring to go on the mission. Now, three weeks later, he couldn't wait to get it over with. He'd already watched just about every sitcom rerun in the Galactic Library and even a new Netflix series of *Lost in Space,* which was made long after he left the planet. It was pretty good, if outdated. He liked the robot.

And speaking of robots, Charlie was slowly changing. It could just be that he was learning—again—from his interactions with Adam, but this seemed to be moving along a lot faster than before. He and Beth were talking, but she was being careful not to dredge up too many lost data files that might shock him too much.

But that wasn't the worst part. Twice on the journey, Charlie had gone dark, the first time for a day, the next time for only two hours. Adam panicked the first time. Without Charlie, his mission would be infinitely more difficult … and dangerous. Adam was on a link with the Formilian techs—they were still on Dizona fitting Galena for her device. They told him this was expected and to be patient. Adam was, but he worried what might happen if, during the operation, Charlie wigged out again. When he came back up, Adam asked him about it. He had no recollection of the lost time.

The next time it happened, Adam monitored it closely. However, two data points did not give him any reference for a developing pattern, no time intervals, and no length of time difference in his recovery. Adam spent the next few days hoping Charlie would go dark again, just so he'd have more information. But that didn't happen by the time Adam reached Racitor.

Adam was considering postponing the mission until Galena linked with him. There was a gala affair being planned sixteen days from now, and Davos had RSVP'd. He didn't have time to postpone anything. Considering travel time, Davos could be leaving any day now.

Beth had already switched out the *Arieel's* transponder code, but just to be sure, Adam landed the starship in a spaceport four hundred miles from the city of Sasorn Mar, where Davos had his headquarters. He'd purchased a large native truck through his surrogates, and it was waiting for him at the spaceport.

Adam quickly loaded the truck and headed out for Sasorn Mar. The *Arieel* lifted on its own and began orbiting, staying fairly close to the tropical sea where the Varisa was located. Fourteen minutes at maximum burn, and the ship could be to the surface, be it water or land.

Racitor was your typical Tier One planet with top-rated technology, a varied climate and ten billion inhabitants. Adam found—much to his chagrin—that Davos was a native of the planet. Knowing how big and strong his brother had been meant Adam wouldn't have too much advantage when fighting the natives—Davos included. But an assassination didn't always mean a physical altercation. In fact, it was a mistake when it came down to that. That being said, Adam still hoped to get his hands around the neck of the mass murderer, the mass murderer of his friends.

Adam had a full array of energy weapons to take to the underwater habitat, along with knives and projection swords. Unfortunately, he'd have to leave his kinetic weapons behind. There would be too much danger of breaching a bulkhead or a pressure window with a bullet. He studied as much as he could about the Racitoreans to find what level of energy bolt it would take to kill them, and he couldn't find much information. He would start with Level-2, but he would be ready to bump it up if need be.

The drive took place mostly at night, so Adam didn't get to see much of the Racitorean landscape. There were dozens of small to medium size towns between where he landed and Sasorn Mar and the traffic was touch and go. In the end, it took six and a half hours to make the trip, which was the most Adam had driven in years if not decades. He kinda liked it. It brought back memories of Earth.

The sun was coming up by the time he entered the city limits of Sasorn Mar. Here, traffic bogged down, taking another forty minutes for Adam to find his warehouse. This was another transaction he consummated long distance from Dizona. It was a typical tilt-up concrete building with a roll-up door. Charlie activated the motors, and the door opened, revealing the other three vehicles Adam had purchased essentially online. They were all smaller panel trucks used by service workers in every city on every civilized planet in the galaxy.

With the door closed again, Adam moved the three packages he had in the back of the larger truck to the vans. Each package looked to be a fifty-five-gallon drum, and Adam secured them to the middle of the cargo area in the vans with tie-down straps before placing electronic devices on the side walls with wires running to the barrels.

They looked like bombs. Which was exactly what they were.

But unlike what Davos had unleashed on Starfire, these bombs were different. At least, Adam hoped they would be.

By this time, Adam had been awake for twenty straight hours, counting the time in the *Arieel* entering the Racitorean star system, plus the landing and the drive to Sasorn Mar. Not surprisingly, he wasn't tired. He was now operating on cloning juice as the thrill of the hunt fully consumed him. His long mission was coming to a close, and he couldn't sleep even if he wanted to. Besides, there was still work to do.

Adam took each van and drove them to their designated parking spaces—spaces he'd leased weeks before, guaranteeing they'd be available. After parking a vehicle, he would take a cab back to the warehouse for another one. All of this took three hours. It was Day-12—noon—by the time he finished.

Now, he did take a break, eating a little and catching an hour of shuteye. He awoke invigorated and ready to start the show.

Adam left the warehouse in the truck and drove to the waterfront. He parked a couple of miles away from the dock where Davos' yacht was moored before donning his SCUBA gear and entering the warm waters at a secluded spot he'd identified from the aerial maps of the region. He had a small, battery-powered underwater scooter shaped like a miniature version of his oxygen tanks but with handles on each side. The scooter could carry him through the water at over eight miles per hour and it had an hour and a half of battery life. In his oversized cargo pack, Adam had an extra battery. The tiny water jet had Formilian circuits in its wireless system so it could be controlled through his ATD. He would leave it at sea as he entered the habitat, but it would be available at a moment's notice if he needed it.

The warm water was clear—almost too clear—requiring Adam to go a little deeper and into the sea reeds along the sandy bottom. The mooring was deep in the marina to accommodate the larger vessels. And there was no vessel larger than Davos', although it was tame by Human standards. Davos had a catamaran-style yacht measuring a hundred feet long by eighty wide. And although it had sails, Adam learned that the boat was equipped with two huge electric motors powered by a 15 MG cold fusion reactor. The few write-ups Adam had seen about the yacht said it was built for speed and stability, not as a sailing vessel.

The Varisa was anchored twenty miles offshore at the edge of a shallow continental shelf and in a coral reef that ran for miles along the shore, similar to the Great Barrier Reef on Earth. Out of curiosity, Adam had looked up the fish life in the seas of Racitor and found striking similarities with Earth's sea life. There was even the deadly, primordial killer, looking remarkably like great whites. There was no improving on perfection, Adam figured. The sharks of Earth didn't survive for five hundred million years for nothing. It was because they were the perfect predators, much like mankind, but not as creative.

Adam gripped the handles of the scooter and activated the motor by mental control. The tiny jet spit out water instantly, and he took off, feeling the rush of the sea against his face and mask. He breathed normally, letting muscle memory take over. He'd always been comfortable in the ocean, having been born and raised in San Diego.

Adam had always planned on joining the Navy, especially the SEALs. As a young teenager, he trained like a SEAL and thought like a SEAL. His father, David, was a Master Chief Petty Officer and encouraged his son's chosen career. But being a SEAL wasn't guaranteed. He received a SEAL challenge contract as a civilian and entered the Navy specifically to train to be a SEAL. After boot camp, he went to the Great Lakes Naval Station for Pre-BUD/S before returning to San Diego for BUD/S training.

Even though Adam had spent the better part of six years preparing for the training, it was still a challenge. Because of that, all graduates felt an overwhelming sense of pride for what they accomplished, even Adam. He came out as a Seaman before being shipped off to Little Creek Naval Amphibious Base in Virginia. He spent his first enlistment, climbing to the rank of Petty Officer Second Class. He'd passed the first-class exam and was on the list for advancement when he was sent on a fateful mission into the Hindu Kush mountains in early January 2011. That mission changed the course of Adam's life, along with that of the Milky Way. Adam often reflected on how such seemingly insignificant events could change history for every living creature in a galaxy. And it all started on a snowy mountain in Pakistan and now led to an underwater wonderland on an alien world forty thousand light-years from Earth.

Adam had let his mind wander as he glided through the water, churning up memories just as he disturbed the myriad of sea life at the bottom of the bay. But now he had to concentrate as he neared the double hulls of the catamaran. Adam surfaced near the portside engine, seeing that the yacht was powered by waterjets and not propellers. He was sure the ship could fly through the water, which was a concern for him. He debated whether or not to ride the hull to the habitat or climb aboard the boat. It would be safer to stay in the water if he could find a place to stay out of the tremendous current. But this was a catamaran. It didn't have long keels, relying on the boat's width to keep it stable while under sail or power. There weren't a lot of places to hide.

But there was a loading port for seacraft on the port pontoon. Adam would make his entrance through there.

Charlie activated the pressure door that lowered down, revealing a spacious interior with two alien jet skis and an assortment of other gear for a variety of watersports. It seemed the super-wealthy mass murderer loved his toys.

Adam scooted inside, moving his heavy bag, including the scooter, in with him. He found an inconspicuous place to stash his gear and himself, removing his fins, mask and scuba gear and then waited. He was ensconced in his hiding place … when he had Charlie detonate the bombs back in town.

16

The vans exploded with an abundance of smoke, fire and noise—especially noise. A minute before the detonations, loud sirens had gone off inside the vans, causing the people around them to run for cover. Adam had researched what alarm sounds would elicit the most reaction from the natives, and according to video from the hovering drones, Adam saw that the klaxons did the trick. When the vans blew, only a few of the natives were knocked off their feet before the real fireworks show started.

And that's what it was, a fireworks show.

After the initial blast of the ammonium nitrate and nitromethane concoction, the tiny amount of the fertilizer-based explosive was enough to blow the back and top of the van apart. Then, the firework mixture that took up the remaining four feet of volume inside the barrels ignited. Adam had mixed the ingredients not to produce the most beautiful explosions high in the sky but to make the most noise and smoke possible. The area around the vans was soon choked with black and grey smoke and filled with a cacophony of mini-explosions. Windows shattered in the three buildings Adam targeted, the three buildings that were the clustered headquarters of Davos Pannel.

Creatures representing a multitude of species panicked and ran from the buildings, knowing for sure that the whole of downtown Sasorn Mar was under attack. And one of those people was Davos Pannel.

He'd been waiting for this moment for far too long, but when it happened, he felt relieved. *And now, let the final battle begin,* Davos chanted as his security team led him from the building and across the street to a waiting hovercopter. The flying craft was always there, serving as a relief valve in case anything like this happened. And now it had.

Davos choked his way through the blinding smoke while half admiring the Human for his tenacity. It had been over eighty days since the battle on Ropor, and finally, his enemy had emerged. As the mogul jumped inside the vehicle and it soared into the sky, Davos thought how this moment verified so much, taking the mystery and uncertainty away.

Yes, the Human had survived the attack on Ropor.

Yes, the Human had learned the true personality behind the attack on the Starfire Building.

And yes, he was here to kill Davos … if Davos didn't kill him first.

And now that this creature—Adam Cain—was on Racitor, Davos would close the net he had established in the city. He knew something like this might happen and that his buildings would be the targets. It was only fitting considering what Davos ordered done in Dal Innis. The only problem is that Davos would not be in the buildings when the Human exacted his revenge. He would be many miles away and safe, safer than any place he would be on land.

He would be at Varisa.

Adam felt stomps of rushing footfalls on the fiberglass—or its alien equivalent—surface of the catamaran, and then seconds later, the motors spun up. Adam could imagine panicked dockworkers barely getting the mooring lines unhooked before the yacht shot off into the open sea.

Adam felt the surge of acceleration from the truly powerful motors, hearing the water race by only millimeters from him through the pontoon hull. The craft was incredibly seaworthy and sliced through the waves with barely a pause. He could hear shouts on deck and in the living compartments as the thirty or so strike force troops settled in for the half-hour race to the habitat. Even traveling at over sixty knots, it was still a good bet that the hovercopter would beat the security detachment to Varisa.

Adam would have preferred for Davos to take the yacht to the habitat, but that wasn't how it would be done in an emergency. The mogul would be evacuated by air and flown to Varisa while the security team followed in the yacht. Since the habitat wasn't constantly manned, there was no need to maintain a security force aboard. But Davos wouldn't go anywhere without one. It only seemed appropriate that Adam would hitch a ride; after all, he was probably going to kill all the people aboard the yacht. This was Adam's way of bonding with them before the killing began. *They'd shared a cruise together,* Adam thought sarcastically.

Adam didn't know why he was feeling so giddy. Was it because his plan was coming together, and he was about to flex his muscles in combat again? After all, he hadn't killed anyone in almost three months. These callous thoughts made him grin, knowing he wasn't serious. It was just his way of lessening the tension as the ship drew closer to its destination. There was still a lot of mission to accomplish for him to let down his guard and get lackadaisical. Nothing was for certain, no matter how meticulously he planned the operation.

He knew this first part was the easy part. Once he got to the habitat, then the real mission would begin. And unfortunately, that part was still a little fuzzy.

. . .

After a while, the motors groaned to silence, and the catamaran came to a rest in the water, swaying from side to side with a gentle rocking motion. Adam savored the moment as the craft taxied to the dock on the anchored tower sitting adjacent to the underwater facility.

The support tower wasn't much more than a metal scaffolding climbing two hundred feet into the air with a cluster of communication antennae and satellite dishes filling a disk-shaped platform on top. Surrounding the tower was a rectangular metal dock with power modules, O2 controls and CO2 scrubbers. Although the habitat was underwater, it wasn't self-sufficient. It relied on external facilities to supply it with electricity, air and water.

Adam felt when the boat touched the dock, and more footfalls were heard scrambling around above him. The dock was on the portside, the same as his hiding place. That would make it easy for him to exit the hold and slip into the water under the dock.

He let the security team leave the catamaran and enter a transfer submersible for the short trip to the habitat. From his research, Adam knew the miniature submarine could only carry ten people at a time, so either it would make multiple trips, or the rest of the strike team would stay on the dock in case they were needed. Adam gave the tiny submarine time to unload its cargo before he prepared to make the dive to the habitat.

His cargo bag was waterproof with its own set of weights to keep it submerged. Now, Adam opened it and began pulling out his gear. His energy weapons had their own waterproof bag, and he would open it once he got to Varisa. But now he took out a tiny rebreather device that was a tube nine inches long and two inches in diameter and equipped with a mouthpiece. This was a container of compressed air that would give him ten minutes of breathing without the need for the bulky buoyancy compensator and air tanks. He would go in with only the rebreather, his mask and the weapons bag.

Charlie, what can you tell me about the hovercopter? Adam asked his ATD.

The craft is on the dock and has been for approximately ten minutes, according to the engine cooling rate.

Adam nodded to himself. That meant Davos was here and had already transferred to Varisa. Good, just where Adam wanted him. He would wait another few minutes to see if the submarine came back for another load of guards. If not, then that would be better. Only ten security personnel to deal with, rather than twenty or more. However, once he was detected aboard the habitat, it would be a sure bet reinforcements would be on the way. But Adam had a plan for that, too.

When the submarine didn't return in a reasonable amount of time, Adam had Charlie open the door to the hold. He slipped down the loading ramp and into the water, pulling his weighted gear bag with him.

Charlie was already busy negating all the enemy energy weapons on the dock, although, with this new version of the A.I., Adam had to command him to do it rather than Charlie doing it on his own. Adam was so used to considering his ATD like another living team member, able to think independently. That wasn't the case anymore. Adam would have to remember that if things get dicey. Charlie won't have his back unless Adam orders him to have his back.

Adam sank to the bottom, skimming along the side of a coral uprising where the tower was anchored. The solid support legs were only about thirty feet deep at this point, and Adam noticed how the undersea topography descended from here to much greater depths. Varisa was visible from here, although still a couple of hundred yards away.

The habitat was made up of three layers of round disks, with the smallest one on top and the largest on the bottom. Each disk was about twenty feet thick and covered along the narrow edge with rows of oblong-shaped windows. The largest and lowest disk sat about one hundred fifty feet below the surface. A series of permanent anchor lines held the habitat to the seafloor. There were forty feet between the lowest disk and the coral seabed, and this was where the tiny submarine was docked.

Adam found very little data about the habitat itself except to know it existed. He had only the rough outside dimensions but knew nothing of the interior. However, he was familiar with these types of structures, having studied them extensively during his Navy days. But that was another lifetime ago and half a galaxy away—literally—and he was a little fuzzy on the details. But he was sure the pressured habitat would have what was called a 'moon room' at its lowest point, where submersibles and personnel could achieve ingress and egress. That was where the submarine was now located, its stout conning tower reaching up in the opening, allowing the security team access to the habitat.

Adam began moving along the radically sloped ocean floor, using the small water scooter for propulsion, gaining depth with every meter he moved. The seafloor was a dazzling circus of coral heads and seagrass teeming with life. Familiar-looking angel fish, smelt and even barracuda watched his progress with unwavering curiosity, sizing up the strange invader to their world. At one point, Adam was startled when a small stingray-like creature shot out from the sand almost directly below him and raced off in a panic. Everything around the Human danced and displayed vivid colors with a rhythmic harmony that permeated the underwater world. The variety of life was astounding, as it was in every coral reef environment Adam had ever experienced. It was stunningly beautiful.

But ahead lay something that was not beautiful, at least to the Human. He was nearing Varisa and the trapped Davos Pannel, even though the alien/native didn't know he was trapped.

Just then, Adam sensed another presence. He dropped to the sandy bottom and looked behind him. Two black beady eyes were locked on him, showing no fear and no curiosity, only assessment. They were the eyes of the apex predator in these waters, an alien shark approaching twenty feet in length.

Like sharks on Earth, this one had to keep moving to breathe, and now it made a leisurely circle of the potential prey, a seal-like creature that promised a satisfying meal. Adam didn't panic. Instead, he withdrew a Ka-Bar knife from a sheath on his utility belt and held it out in front of him. Sharks don't normally attack divers, and he knew how to ward them off. But he couldn't spend much time here. His rebreather was rapidly running out of air.

Adam cautiously began swimming away, twisting as he did to keep the shark in sight. Then, the primordial creature did something unexpected. It disappeared. The grey skin of the fish suddenly warbled and turned translucent, showing its internal organs. At the same time, it dislocated its bottom jaw, looking like an earthmover ready to scoop up a large pile of dirt. But in this case, Adam was the dirt.

Normally, a good hit to the snout would rattle the cartilage in the shark's head, disorienting the creature and sending it scurrying away. But Adam couldn't see the snout. It had folded back on itself, making the mouth even larger, a looming rectangle that was visible only by the three rows of pyramid-shaped white teeth.

With one hand on the scooter and the other holding the knife, Adam sent a mental command to gun the water jet. The tiny device pulled Adam to the side just as the wavering translucent form sped past. Then, with a quick jerk of his arm, Adam shoved the tip of the Ka-Bar into the underside of the shark. Instantly, the fish spasmed and sent a powerful surge of water from its caudal fin into Adam's face. The flip of its tail fin was enough to shoot it away in the blink of an eye, trailing blood as it went. The shark disappeared over the edge of the underwater embankment.

Adam sucked in another deep breath through the rebreather. The next breath didn't come. He was out of air.

Grasping desperately at his utility belt, Adam pulled out his backup unit, his last one and quickly shoved it between his lips. He took in a deep, welcoming breath. After a moment to catch his wits, Adam lined up on the Varisa again. It was still a hundred feet away, maybe more. He looked across the seafloor, spotting his previously discarded equipment bag. Aiming the scooter in that direction, Adam didn't even slow down as he reached with his left hand and grabbed the netting covering the bag.

The bag was a drag on his forward progress, slowing him down considerably. He paced his breathing, trying to preserve as much air as he could in the rebreather.

As he neared the habitat, he slowed down even more, being aware of the multiple lights and cameras aimed at the underwater wonderland around it. Would those within the structure be sightseeing at the moment, or would they be securing their subject and watching video feeds of the scene back in Sasorn Mar? Either way, Adam had to be careful as he slid up beside the small transfer submarine, careful to avoid the forward viewport at the base of the squat conning tower.

Above him, Adam saw the lighted moon pool, looking like a turbulent bowl of shimmering mercury. He slowly approached the surface until he could see through the rippling water to the room beyond. There was a figure up there, moving across Adam's line of sight and heading for an open hatchway. But he didn't go through. Instead, he stopped and began punching buttons on a wall module. Then he punched them some more.

Growing impatient, Adam hooked the equipment bag on part of the lining to the moon pool before carefully lifting his head out of the water, his eyes never moving from the huge native who now had his back to Adam. The Human removed the rebreather and placed it in a pouch on his utility belt, with his right hand returning to the surface holding the black-bladed Ka-Bar knife.

There was a short ladder extending into the water from the pool, and Adam moved over to it. He removed his mask and set it on the deck just above the waterline. Then he climbed out of the pool.

There was plenty of ambient sound in the room, including the sloshing of water, along with constant pressure popping. It was like that in all underwater habitats. It was seldom quiet. The noise helped mask Adam's emergence from the water, and his bare feet muffled his footsteps as he moved up behind the guard.

The creature was seven feet tall, with broad shoulders and a thick neck. Even for his size, the head was huge and topped with a crop of spongy black hair in tight curls. He wore a grey uniform with creases under the fabric, which made Adam suspect he wore a diffusion shield underneath. Hopefully, that was just SOP and not a sign that the guards were expecting action inside the habitat. This was supposed to be Davos' sanctuary, the place where he didn't think he could be attacked.

As he expected, the guard sensed Adam's presence when the Human was still about four feet away. Now, Adam jumped forward, aiming his blade for the middle of the alien's back, along where the spine would be. At the same time, he made a little jump so he could reach the top of the Racitorean's shoulder and wrapped his left arm around his neck. The guard placed his arms against the bulkhead and shoved, sending him and Adam backward. He stumbled with Adam's weight on his back and from the agonizing pain as his spine was severed. The guard fell back on top of Adam, grabbing the arm around his neck at the same time he attempted to yell out.

After the quick thrust into the alien's back, Adam had withdrawn the blade and brought his right arm up. Now, he expertly ran the edge across the throat of the guard, cutting off his ability to call for help. Blood flowed, and air gurgled from the wound.

Adam shoved the huge alien off of him and stood up. Without hesitation, Adam stepped over to where he'd hooked the weapons bag. He reached into the water and pulled it out, already kneeling and working the seals.

Adam had three MK-88s, along with ten power packs. That should be enough. But he also had a Xan-fi J-4, a compact close-quarters weapon with a shorter barrel than the standard N-1. He had four power packs for this weapon since it could fire twenty Level-1 bolts on a single charge. There was a carrying strap on the weapon, and Adam strung it around his neck, cradling the weapon across his chest. His utility belt didn't have holsters; instead, he had Velcro-like strips on which he placed the MKs. Then he filled both the utility belt pouches, as well as the chest pockets in his mesh shirt, with the ten MK power packs. Each weapon already had a fully charged pack inserted.

Adam had a pair of Ka-Bars on his belt, and now he slipped his trusty projection sword into a loop on his right hip. When he stood, Adam was ready for action.

Charlie, give me a reading on where the guards are. Adam asked in his mind, knowing he had to ask before the data would be displayed. He tensed when all he felt was … nothing. He was talking to himself. *Charlie, are you there?*

Adam then tried to access his ATD the old-fashioned way, simply by concentrating. It still didn't work. His ATD was dead.

17

"Shit," Adam muttered to himself. Now what? Had Charlie disarmed the weapons in the habitat before he died, as he had done on the tower dock? Adam wouldn't know until the first contact.

This changed his tactics. If all the MKs had been disabled, Adam could have simply waltzed throughout the habitat, taking out bad guys without a worry. Now, he had to be more careful.

Adam headed for the hatch from the moon room. This was the lowest disk and the largest. Since Adam hadn't found schematics for the habitat itself, he wasn't sure how the living arrangements were set up, but he could guess. This lower section could be used for living quarters for the guards and servant crew. The corridors would be circular to follow the curvature of the disk, with staterooms and other compartments radiating out from there. There would be a central ladder or elevator leading up to the higher and smaller disks.

Considering who owned Varisa, Adam had to assume the other two disks would be reserved for Davos. He saw that the upper disk was made up of almost all windows, affording a 360-degree view of the outside world. It was small enough to form one large room, with side seating and maybe even a dining area for Davos and his guests. It would be a spectacular scene, with the lights shining within the coral and a ballet of neon-colored fish providing the entertainment.

That would leave the middle disk for Davos' living quarters, for him and his distinguished guests. That meant that the bulk of the guards and service staff would be located in the lower disk, the one Adam was in.

Early on, Adam had decided to limit his action to eliminating Davos and not his entire organization. Of course, that meant taking out his closest security shield in the process. He knew that he couldn't simply find Davos, kill him, and then get away cleanly. There had to be considerable collateral damage. After all, what would an Adam Cain mission be without a lot of collateral damage?

But did Adam want to start off with the security team, or did he want to start with Davos? Unfortunately, the decision was not up to him. And without his ATD working, he was walking into the dark. He would have to take things as they came.

Adam entered a quickly curving corridor with doorways to both the left and right. The disk was only large enough for one corridor. The outside would be the staterooms and compartments with portholes. The inner compartments would be for food prep and other services. Since utilities came in from outside, there was no need to have large oxygen units or scrubbers and batteries to run the electronics.

Fortunately, no one was in the corridor. With only one submarine of security and service personnel moved from the dock, the most there could be in Varisa would be ten people, plus Davos and whomever he brought with him in the hovercopter. The structure could easily accommodate that many people, and perhaps the newly arrived guards were in their staterooms, stowing their gear. Adam didn't look the gift horse in the mouth for long; instead, he moved quickly along the corridor until he came to a crossing passageway that he saw reached through to the other side of the disk, joining again with the main corridor. In the center was a circular stairway going up.

So far, so good. Adam began climbing the stairway.

In a buffer space between disks, Adam came to a landing and a pressure door. This made sense, as it was a way to protect each disk from a catastrophic loss of integrity in the others. There would be a similar door leading to the top section.

Adam had only taken three more steps up the ladder when the lower pressure door suddenly cycled closed. At the same time, the one above him did the same, trapping him in the middle disk.

And that's when guards appeared down both lengths of the central corridor. Half of them were crouched down on one knee with other members of the team standing behind them. All had MKs pointed in his direction.

If his ATD had been working, Adam would know whether or not the weapons were active. But since Charlie was taking an ill-timed nap, he had no way of knowing. Adam pulled his hands away from the Xan-fi, holding them out to his side. It was obvious Davos was expecting him.

Guards rushed up to him and began disarming him, with the native directly in front of him frowning as he and his cohorts kept pulling more and more weapons off Adam's body. Then the security boss pursed his lips and nodded his approval, one professional to another.

Then the upper pressure hatch cycled open, and, with a smile, the senior guard motioned for Adam to continue up the stairway.

Not surprisingly, a gleeful Davos Pannel was in the room, seated comfortably on a curving double-sided white couch, with one seating arrangement facing into the circular room and the other side facing out at the seascape beyond the windows. There was another civilian in the room, standing to one side at a beverage bar. He had a drink in his hand. Three guards accompanied Adam into the room and took up positions evenly spaced along the perimeter. Fortunately, no one seemed in a hurry to kill the Human, so Adam relaxed and went with the flow. He motioned toward the bar.

"Do you mind if I get a drink? I think I'm going to need it."

Davos raised his own glass and nodded. The civilian stepped away, and the smiling lead guard moved to the counter with Adam.

"What would you like?" the guard asked with humor.

"Something that won't kill me."

The guard smiled even more. "There are not many things in Varisa that will not. But I will use my discretion." He looked to Davos, who nodded.

The guard poured Adam a thick caramel-color drink. Adam caught a familiar whisp, catching himself before he asked if this was *flasia*. A person of Adam's caste would not know of the drink, not unless Galena had given it to him. Adam sighed, knowing he'd dodged a bullet. Metaphorically, of course.

Adam sipped the drink, doing his part to gush over the exquisite taste and fragrance.

"It is certainly a drink to die for," Davos said with a laugh. "Which, in your case, is exactly what is going to happen."

The other civilian stepped over to a side chair and sat down.

"Let us introduce ourselves," said Davos. "I am Davos Pannel. To my left is Cranis Capola, the First Supervisor of the Sylos Syndicate. And serving the drinks is Vigis Mor Solois, the commander of my security force and the person who convinced me that you might try something like this. Congratulations, Vigis; you win the bet."

Adam sipped more of the *flasia*, making sure he got all he could if this was to be his last drink. Davos was right; it was to die for. Adam finished the glass and held it out for another. With an even more wicked grin, Vigis obliged.

"So, you are the famous Adam Cain," Davos said, toasting his glass to Adam. "That is right, my friends. Before us stands a wonder of science and magic, the first person to certifiably be brought back from the dead. Once I learned this fact—and that you were truly him—I questioned whether you were immortal or not, much like your mutant friends. But then I decided you were not. Of course, I still cannot be sure, no matter my beliefs. Today, I will have my answer."

"May I sit down?" Adam asked, moving from the bar and more to the center of the room. He was suddenly feeling weary.

"You may not!" Davos announced. "You are wet, and you will ruin the fabric."

"So will my blood."

Davos looked at Vigis. "He has a point. Let us make sure it will be a bloodless death. It is hard to get cleaners out to Varisa."

Adam leaned his wet butt against another chair, causing Davos to bristle. "Look, I want to tell you I didn't mean to kill your brother," Adam began. "All I was doing was making an arrest. He resisted. And when we fell off the building, I was trying to save him, not kill him. He was worth more money to me alive than dead."

A dark cloud came over Davos' face. He cocked his head.

"Which brother?" the mogul asked.

Adam was taken aback by the question. "Daxian," he stammered.

Davos laughed. "Daxian!" he looked at Cranis Capola. "Is he dead?"

Cranis nodded. "He died on Calinan." The alien looked at Adam. "Apparently, he fell off a building to his death. I am sure I told you about it."

Davos waved a hand. "Perhaps you did." He looked at Adam. "What does my brother have to do with anything? Are you telling me you were there when he died?"

"You didn't know that?" Adam asked incredulously.

"It is the first I am hearing of this … or not. I cannot remember." The tone of Davos' voice left no doubt he was telling the truth.

"I thought the whole reason you bombed the Starfire Building was because you thought I killed your brother."

Davos laughed, as did Cranis Capola. "I care not when a brother dies. Especially Daxian. I never liked him."

"I sent him to Calinan to keep him away from Syndicate business," said Cranis. "He was an embarrassment, always getting in trouble with the law. I take it that was why you attempted an arrest?"

Adam nodded.

"And now you think I bombed Starfire … for revenge?" said Davos.

"Well, he was your brother."

"Humans must have very different familial ties than do Racitoreans. I have seventeen brothers and ten sisters. I cannot keep track of all of them. They go about their lives with very little contact. Daxian, however, was a nuisance. If you killed him, then I thank you."

Adam didn't give a damn if he had permission or not. He moved around the chair and sat down, wet clothes and all.

"If you didn't bomb the building because of Daxian, then why did you bomb it?"

"For the only reason anyone does anything. I was paid to do it."

"Paid! By whom?"

Davos frowned and waved his hand again. "What does it matter? It is done. Besides, it was more of a favor than anything else."

"Who was it!" Adam yelled.

Davos recoiled while Vigis took a step toward Adam. The mogul waved back his security chief.

"You feel very passionate about this, I can tell. And is that the reason you came after Salwan and now me? Why?"

Adam couldn't believe the cavalier and dismissive attitude of the Racitorean. "Why? Because you killed hundreds of my friends, innocents who didn't deserve to die. You can't see that?"

"I suppose that would be motivation … for some."

"For anyone with a heart. Are you that much of a psychopath not to care?"

"A moment as the translator defines 'psychopath.'" Davos suddenly raised his eyebrows. "That is an interesting definition. I like it. I shall have to adopt it for my own."

"You truly are crazy," Adam said. He felt drained and near the point of collapse. He had come this far to face the person ultimately responsible for the killing of his friends, just to learn there was still another. This was exhausting.

"I will let you continue with your insults since you will not have much time to savor them."

"Tell me … who wanted the building bombed?"

"Again, what does it matter? You cannot take the knowledge to the aftertime." Davos laughed. "Or perhaps you can, Adam Cain. All right, I will tell you. Handal Owiss."

Adam frowned. "Who is Handal Owiss?"

Davos cocked his head. "You live on Tel'oran, and you do not know who Handal Owiss is?"

"I don't know," Adam said. "Maybe. It sounds a little familiar."

"He is but one of your governing counselors."

"A politician!"

"Correct. A politician with ambitions."

"What do you mean?" Adam gasped.

"He seeks to eventually be the leader of the planet—its president. Currently, he is on the council, facing reelection. Apparently, he has competition he did not trust he could defeat. And only a councilmember can be elevated to president."

"Tidus!" Adam called out.

Davos again recoiled from Adam's intensity.

"What is a Tidus?" Davos asked.

"He is a Juirean, the head of Starfire Security," Vigis answered for Adam. Being in the security business, he had heard of Tidus Fe Nolan.

"You work for a Juirean … but you are a Human?"

"Yes, I do, and I'm proud of that."

Davos shrugged. "It is none of my concern."

"You tried to kill him," Adam charged.

"Then he still lives?" Davos said, looking over at Cranis with mock shock on his face. "Then our friend Handal will be very disappointed with us. If the purpose of the bombing was to kill the Juirean, then we have failed in our duty. I may have to refund the fee to Handal. It is the least I can do."

Then Davos turned his green eyes on Adam again. "But first, we must deal with you, Human. I am sad to say that our time is now over. I have so enjoyed our talk. It has been illuminating. And now I have learned that Daxian is dead."

"I already told you that before," Cranis corrected.

Davos waved a dismissive hand. "Whatever."

Adam, it is I ... Charlie.

Adam recoiled sharply, almost yelling out loud when he heard the voice in his head. *Charlie! I'm so glad to hear you again.*

What has been happening? I have only fragments of memories. Where are we, and how is Beth and David?

Adam let out a deep sigh, which was mistaken by Davos and the others as a sigh of surrender. But that wasn't the case. Adam was just getting ready to fight.

What do you last remember? Adam asked mentally.

We were on Ropor, then only fragments, as I said. But a quick survey of my systems and backup files shows I am in full working order. I appeared to have gone through a realignment. But that will have to wait. I have scanned the recent recordings of the previous conversation. It appears you are in considerable danger. Are you aware there are numerous activated energy weapons in the area, including in this room?

Yeah, I was aware of that. Is there anything you can do to help me out?

That is a silly question. Of course, there is. I will start with the energy weapons in this room.

Adam grinned widely, catching Davos off guard. "You seem relieved at the prospect of your death. I suppose for you, it is nothing new. However, this time, it will surely be permanent. Vigis, if you will do the honors. And please do not stain the carpet or the furniture."

Vigis approached Adam with an MK in his hand. "Do not resist. I will stun you first and then strangle the life from your body. It will be painless."

"Wow, that's really nice of you, Vigis. Maybe when this is over, you can come to work for me at Starfire. I kinda like you."

Vigis pursed his lips. "Farewell, Adam Cain."

The alien lifted his weapon and pointed it at Adam's chest. A stun bolt was more effective with a body shot as it affected the heart and nervous system. The problem for Vigis: His weapon wasn't working. He pressed the trigger once, twice, three times.

Adam sat quietly in the chair, looking up at the seven-foot-tall Racitorean, a peaceful smile on his face.

"What is wrong?" Davos asked, sitting up straighter on the couch.

"I do not know. The weapon has malfunctioned."

"Then get another!"

Vigis strode over to one of the other two guards and took his weapon. It was an MK-88. He returned to Adam, who was still sitting nonchalantly in the chair. He pointed the weapon at Adam and pulled the trigger, letting out an angry roar when the weapon didn't fire. Then he twisted the level setting nob, first to Level-2 and then to Level-1. Still nothing.

"What is happening here?" Vigis yelled, glaring down at Adam.

"You will find all your weapons are dead. Let me prove it to you."

Adam sprung to his feet and pulled the inert weapon from Vigis's hand. The remaining armed guard had his weapon pointed at Adam, frantically pulling the trigger but with the same result.

Vigis wasn't afraid. The weapon was dead; all the weapons were dead. They could cause him no harm. And that was when Adam placed a Level-1 bolt into the security chief's chest.

"Oops," said Adam. "I was mistaken. This one seems to be working. Oh, and by the way, the job offer is rescinded."

Adam now spun on the other two guards and laid them out with center-mass shots at Level-1. Then it was onto Cranis. The Syndicate executive had dived behind the chair, while Davos did the same at the couch. An alarm sounded, telling Adam that either the room was under surveillance or Davos had set off a panic button. Solid footfalls could be heard rushing up the spiral staircase from below just as Charlie activated the pressure door leading to the upper observation disk, cycling it shut.

Adam walked slowly toward the couch. Davos was cowering behind it, with Cranis poking his head out from behind the chair, looking to see if Adam was coming after him. Without breaking stride, Adam reached out his right hand and fired a bolt into Cranis's forehead. As it was with Level-1 bolts to the head, the star-hot plasma boiled the brain, creating a pressure build-up that caused the head to explode.

"Oh, damn," Adam said. "Sorry about the carpet. Just send me the cleaning bill."

Before Adam knew it, Davos sprung over the couch with lightning-quick reflexes, landing his seven-foot-tall frame on the much shorter and smaller Human. The move caught Adam off guard, as the Human was more caught up with killing Cranis and his witty remarks than keeping his attention focused on the mogul.

Like his brother, Davos had some solid weight behind him, and Adam fell to the carpeted floor as the vicious native tore into him. The MK slipped from his hand and slid under the couch. Then the Human took two quick punches to the rib cage, knocking the air from his lungs, followed by a crushing blow to the side of his head. Sparkles appeared before Adam's eyes, and his mind was shocked by the sudden turn of events.

What the hell! Adam thought. *Humans aren't supposed to get beat up.* What kind of bizzarro world was he in?

Then Adam shook off the cobwebs in time to twist his head away from another crushing blow to his head. He reached up and grabbed both of Davos' wrists. He squeezed, as he'd done a hundred times before, expecting the alien to cry out in pain. But Davos didn't. Instead, he jerked his arms to the side, breaking Adam's grip, then swept his double-clenched fists across Adam's face.

The blow was so powerful that it rolled Adam onto his side, which probably saved his life. Adam continued to roll until Davos fell off of him. But, as Adam tried to crawl away, Davos clamped down on his bare ankles, pulling Adam back to him. Adam's clothing was still wet, dripping just enough moisture down his legs as he sat in the chair to make the Human's skin slippery. Davos broke his grip, allowing Adam to bend his right knee up and then extend the heel of his foot into the alien's face.

Davos toppled backward, suffering from the first real hit Adam landed on the native. But now the dynamics of the fight changed as Adam managed to get to his feet, squaring up against the towering creature.

"Are you done playing around?" Adam asked with false bravado. To tell the truth, he was still a little wobbly, and his vision blurred. He could feel the cloning juice surging through his body, bringing welcome relief. Still, it would take a minute or so for him to fully regain his senses.

Davos was having a hard time himself. He'd taken a solid kick to his face, and blood gushed from a broken nose. He flicked the red liquid from his face with a trembling hand before snarling at Adam.

Adam wasn't much better. Blood trailed down the side of his head from his left ear, and his lip was badly cut. But unlike Davos, Adam was already on the mend. The cloning juice was like a strong stimulant, and the fog was already lifting from his brain.

Adam moved to his side, stepping into the center of the circular room like it was an arena.

"Just you and me now, Davos," Adam teased. "Man against Racitorean. A question: If your race is so badass, why haven't you conquered the galaxy ... like the Humans did?"

Davos smiled. "Are you that naive? I *have* conquered the galaxy. I am of a caste that controls everything. You have not heard of us because we do not let you know about us, about how you and everyone else are but slaves to our every whim. I can destroy economies simply because I wish to. I finance wars, and I trade planets as if they were game pieces on a board. I can even wave my hand like that, and a building collapses on Tel'oran. I have killed millions, and yet still I walk free. Why? Because I am above it all."

"Yeah, that's what my good friend Galena Gar told me. She also told me about your unwritten rule about taking a direct hand in the atrocities you order. She said when you bombed the Starfire Building, you broke that code. And that is why she turned you over to me. She said she wanted to excise you from The Community before you smelled up the whole place. And when you're gone, she will swoop in and take over all your holdings. You see, I'm the living embodiment of something we call entropy. It's a Human word that means the change from order to chaos.

What I do to you today will bring chaos to the Syndicate, and then Galena will step in and take it over. All you have built will be gone. And all because you did a favor for a politician on Tel'oran. Oh, and thanks for that information, by the way. It will come in handy."

Davos blinked several times as he attempted to digest the information. But then his face turned defiant again.

"You are assuming that you can best me."

"Of course, I can best you, dickhead. I'm *The Human*. Or were you not paying attention?"

And with that, Adam took a lightning-quick step in toward Davos, sending a left jab into his already broken face. He followed up with a blindingly fast right hook that sent Davos to the floor. Adam wasn't holding back. All the anger and pain of watching the Starfire Building collapse came rushing back. And then the images of Siri experiencing the double pain of losing her child and Vinset. And then the image of his friend and mentor Tidus, a respirator stuck down his throat and the slow, steady bleep of the alien EEG showing minimal brainwaves.

And all because someone didn't want to lose a fucking election.

Adam fell on top of the dazed alien and placed the thick neck in a headlock, clamping down hard on the side of the neck where arteries fed the brain. Every Prime creature had them, although the location shifted from species to species. Adam didn't care. He squeezed, tighter than was necessary to suffocate the brain. That wouldn't be enough. It wouldn't be enough until Adam felt the neck snap and the life flow from the alien mass murderer.

Adam pushed the lifeless body away and leaned against the white couch, now stained with blood. He looked at Davos, feeling a sense of satisfaction if not completion. The *power* behind the bombing was dead, but not the *person* who set everything in motion. As he sat there, Adam wondered what connection Handal Owiss had with Davos. Why would someone like Davos even bother with a low-level politician like him, and on a far distant planet like Tel'oran?

Adam didn't have an answer. Not yet.

The Human recovered two of the flash weapons and then moved to the pressure door between levels. There was constant banging and shouts from the other side as the guards were still trying to open the hatch. But Charlie wasn't letting them.

Now, Adam instructed him to open it.

There was panic on the other side as the guards backed away, expecting Davos to be staring down at them. Instead, it was a smiling Adam Cain. MKs were lifted, and triggers fingered, but nothing happened. Eyes shifted from their inert weapons to the barrels of the two MKs Adam had pointed into the cluster of aliens on the stairs. Then, as a unit, they turned to go back down. And that was when Adam opened fire.

He wasn't subtle about it. His head hurt, and he was pretty sure his left eardrum was punctured. It was still oozing blood even after the rest of his injuries had stopped flowing. Methodically, he moved down the stairs, shooting anyone he saw. As he moved into the lower ring, he began to come upon natives dressed in pale yellow jackets. Adam let them live; they were servants, not soldiers.

With his injured ear, Adam didn't want to reenter the water. So, he took the mini-sub instead. Of course, he had no idea how to pilot the vessel, but that was what his ATD was good for, tracing control modules and activating circuits. Soon, Adam was heading out to sea, not to the tower dock. He would head out a few miles and then call down the *Arieel*. He didn't feel like fighting the other twenty guards who had remained on the dock. He was tired, and he just wanted to rest and heal. And a chilled Diet Pepsi sure would hit the spot right about now.

18

It was Solstice Day on Tel'oran, the celebration of the new season across the planet. For both natives and aliens alike living on the world, it was a pretty big deal. Since they didn't have a Christmas or Bastille Day, it was like having New Year's Eve twice a year. Any excuse to party, right?

All the finest in Dal Innis were present for the celebrations. Since the city was the capital of Tel'oran, government officials were out doing their part, hosting events, MCing others and generally out rubbing elbows with their subjects, even if their *subjects* didn't consider them as such. But that was the attitude of most elected officials. *You put me in charge, so I'm going to rule, not govern.* It was a subtle difference but significant in the minds of some.

Handal Owiss moved through a crowd of supporters, patting him on the back and congratulating him on his recent electoral victory. Another six years on the Council should position him perfectly for the Presidency. He'd already formed an advisory committee to help chart the path, and not even the other council members seemed anxious to challenge him. Besides Tactori, Tel'oran was the second-most powerful planet in the galaxy, and as its President, Handal would be in a position to sit on the Affiliation's Governing Council, with the next step to First Counsellor. That would make Handal the default ruler of the galaxy, the most powerful being in existence.

And it was also Solstice Day! Another cause for celebration. Yes, Handal Owiss was feeling good, proud and successful.

Handal passed through the crowd and into his governing residence in the center of Dal Innis. He had several other residences scattered around the planet, but this was where he spent his time when the Council was in session. It was close to Innin Hall, plus several of the best restaurants in Dal Innis, at least for those who could afford it.

Handal smiled as he entered the warm, wood-paneled hallway leading to the main living area. Most members of his family had sought wealth and power through a variety of means, but none of them had a direct path to control of the galaxy, at least not in the open. Handal would show them all—

Owiss' mate was standing at the end of the hallway, a

look of grave concern on her strong features. He frowned as he approached her and then followed her clouded gaze into the living room. There were people there, mostly Tel'oran, but with a sprinkling of aliens, as well. And prominent among the aliens was his nemesis, the Juirean Tidus Fe Nolan.

Although Tidus had not been in any condition to challenge Handal for his seat, he had heard about the Juirean's miraculous recovery after the bombing of the Starfire Building. That was of little concern now that the election was over. Even if Tidus ran for office again, he would be replacing another council member with a different election cycle. Handal's position would be secure.

But what was the Juirean doing here and with members of the Tel'oran Special Police Force?

"Councilmember Owiss," said an officer Handal knew as Clayus Bax, "we wish to speak with you. Will you now come along with us." It was a statement, not a question.

"What is the meaning of this; what is this inquiry?"

"There have been allegations made against you concerning the bombing of the Starfire Building."

"What kind of allegations?"

"Serious allegations," Tidus Fe Nolan said, stepping forward. The Juirean and the Racitorean stood eye-to-eye, both seven feet tall. "Allow me to use a Human phrase, you son-of-a-bitch. We know what you did."

Handal's heart throbbed in his chest. How could they have found out?

"I know not what you are referencing. You believe I had something to do with the tragedy that befell your company? That is ridiculous." He looked to the police officer. "Where are such allegations originating?"

"Oh, I had a hand in that," said a new voice coming from a much shorter, pink-skinned creature who had been hidden among the taller natives and aliens. Handal didn't need an introduction; he knew who the speaker was.

"I met a relative of yours a while back," said Adam Cain—the Human. Handal knew his true identity, having learned it from others who were better connected to the affairs of the galaxy. "He had some very interesting things to say about you."

"And who would that be?"

"Why, your brother, Davos Pannel, of course."

"My brother?" Handal stammered. "I have no brother named Davos Pannel."

The Human nodded. "You are right. You don't have a brother named Davos Pannel … anymore. That's because he's dead. It didn't take a genius to see the connection immediately. You and Davos are both Racitoreans, and Davos said he had seventeen estranged brothers. Each of you set out into the galaxy, assuming other names and seeking your path to fame and fortune. Some of you succeeded, some didn't. And you have, coming to a planet that allows aliens to seek elected office. And now you have your sights set on the First Counsellor position in the Affiliation. Of course, you had to be selected President of

Tel'oran first, and unfortunately, a pesky—yet popular—Juirean was standing in your way. So, you called your brother and asked a favor: Could you make the Starfire Building disappear?"

"Again, that is ridiculous," Handal charged. "Completely baseless ... and unproven. What evidence could you possibly have as to my involvement in such a horrific event?"

He looked desperately to his mate, who was now standing across the room, her mouth open and her eyes accusatory.

"You cannot possibly believe these lies?" he said to her. "All they have are stories, fantasies."

"Oh, and we do have this," said the Human as he held up a datapad.

Handal glared at the offending device, petrified over what it might contain. He didn't have to wait long to find out. The Human began the device.

"This is a recording captured by a special piece of equipment I had on me at the time. It has both audio and video of Davos naming you as the mastermind of the Starfire bombing."

The recording began, showing a video from a particular point of view as if it came from an eye camera. Knowing that the Human was in the security business, it was not hard to imagine how this could have been achieved. And there was his brother, Davos, clear as day, naming Handal, detailing how and why he had ordered—requested—the bombing of Starfire.

"That is not proof!" Handal cried. "All I did was ask. Davos did not have to oblige. It is his fault, not mine."

Officer Clayus stepped forward and took Handal by the arm. He was too shocked to resist. "That is not how we look at it," said Clayus. "There was also consideration passed between parties. We found evidence of such a transfer in your financial records." Shackles were put on Handal's wrists. "Now, come along with us, former Councilmember Owiss. This nightmare of yours is just beginning."

Adam and Tidus met Inspector Clayus outside the house while a still-protesting Handal Owiss was placed in a patrol car. His wife was at the door screaming at him so vehemently that Adam's translator couldn't keep up.

Tidus put a huge hand on Clayus's shoulder. The Juirean looked weary, having only been released from the hospital two days before. Still, his recovery was miraculous.

"Thank you for doing this, Inspector," said Tidus. "It is good to finally have closure."

"We must still follow up with the remnants of the terror cell," said the police officer. "There is a character known as Rafis, who is their leader. He has fled into the hinterlands. He cannot leave the planet, so we will have him soon." Clayus gave him a concerned look. "Do you still plan to pursue a career in politics?"

Tidus laughed. "If I were wise, I would not. But wisdom is not my strong point. Yes, I will be mounting another campaign once things are back in order with Starfire."

"And what are the plans for your company?"

"To rebuild, of course. I have recently secured financing for an entirely new Starfire Building. Construction should begin soon. And Unidor is still offering us business, even more than before. They are quite impressed at how quickly we brought this matter to a close, with your thanks, Inspector."

Clayus looked embarrassed, meeting Adam's eyes. "I think it disingenuous for me to take more credit than I deserve. I know I was resistant at first, rejecting your offer to help. But looking at what I know of the events over the past few months, I can see where extra-judicial steps were taken." He held up a hand to stop Adam's protest. "Extra-judicial, however effective, and perhaps the only way the matter could have been resolved. And now I hope you will accept me as a friend and colleague. I am sure our paths will cross again. We should always remember, however, that we are all on the same side."

Adam grinned widely. "The eternal battle of good versus evil, right against wrong?"

"I detect sarcasm in your voice, Adam Cain."

"Maybe a little. Sometimes, the lines get blurred; they

have to be to get anything done. A very wise friend told me recently that sometimes laws must be broken, rewritten or circumvented. Circumstances will dictate which."

"Just be careful, my Human friend, as you walk that particular tightrope."

"Always, Inspector. That's the story of my life."

"Which one?"

EPILOGUE

Tidus insisted on returning to the office—in the old Starfire Building—after Handal was arrested. Adam tried to get him to go home and to stay there for as long as it took for him to get back to one hundred percent, but the Juirean was hearing none of it. He insisted he was feeling stronger by the minute, but Adam got the feeling he was just imitating Adam's boasting when his cloning juice did its thing. Tidus only received a small dose of cloning juice. It brought him out of the coma and set him on the path to recovery but at a much slower pace than Adam. However, the Juirean's metabolism was different from the Human's. Maybe he *was* getting more of a jolt out of the concoction.

And speaking of the concoction, the doctors at the hospital were expanding their research center now that they had made a breakthrough with Tidus. Adam was both happy and sad. It was good that he was able to help his friend, but he was worried about what kind of publicity might come his way if the origin of the miracle cure was ever made known. He would have to make sure that knowledge never saw the light of day.

Tidus now squeezed behind a temporary desk that had been brought into his old office. The extravagant stone desk from Juir was now crumpled dust still being cleared from the demolition site of the former Starfire Building. The remaining part of the structure was too badly damaged to be salvageable, so it was razed. Now, native construction crews were working feverishly to clear the debris away for the new edifice that would rise from the ashes of the old.

Titus had grand plans, seeing that he'd recently acquired three other sites next to and across the street from his old building. The other structures had also been damaged in the explosion, and the Juirean picked them up for a song. He now had visions for a revitalized downtown Dal Innis, anchored by the new Phoenix Business Park. No one on the planet except Adam and Tidus understood the meaning of Phoenix in this context. Adam was touched that Tidus would name it after a mythical Human bird.

Even so, Adam was amazed at how fast things were moving on Tel'oran. The bombing occurred only a little over six months before, and in another year, there would be a whole new Starfire Security Building, along with the subsequent company. Tidus seemed to be rolling in dough at the moment.

"Thank God for insurance," Adam said as he removed two Diet Pepsis from Tidus's office refrigerator. The Juirean had acquired a taste for the beverage, even though the carbonation made his eyes water like he was crying. Again, the image of a crying Juirean was so incongruous. But then again, Humans cry, too … a lot.

Tidus sipped the drink and hiccupped. That was something both Human and Juirean had in common as the first trace of carbonation hit their throats.

"Insurance. I wish that was all it took," he began. "I have been fighting with the companies for months. Yes, I could have the cost of the building reimbursed, but then my new premiums would be impossible to pay going forward."

Adam recoiled slightly. "So, what are you going to do?"

"I'm not taking their money, that's what."

Adam waved a symbolic hand around the room. "Then where are you getting the money for all this, for the new complex."

A cloud came over Tidus's face. "That is a sorry subject." He looked at a clock on the wall. "But soon you will have your answer."

At precisely Day-16, the door to Tidus's office opened,

and a familiar figure walked in. Adam nearly fell out of his chair when he saw who it was.

"Galena!" he gasped, jumping to his feet. "What ... what are you doing here?"

The purple-skinned beauty stepped up to him and brushed a light kiss across his lips. Then she proceeded purposefully, pulling a chair up to the desk.

Adam, my love, I have missed you.

Adam heard the words, not aloud but in his mind. He knew Galena had been fitted with an ATD. Now, she seemed quite proficient with it.

Adam ignored the shock of Galena's mental connection, instead looking sharply at Tidus and then back to Galena. "You didn't ... did you?"

Galena smiled. "Of course I did. This is what I do. I find opportunities in chaos, and what has been more chaotic on Tel'oran recently than the untimely bombing of the Starfire Building."

Adam turned to Tidus. "What have you done?"

Tidus displayed an ugly Juirean grimace. "I did what I had to do. Now, Adam, sit. It is not as bad as you think."

Adam hesitated a moment, debating whether to sit or to flee. It wasn't that he didn't respect Galena and her business acumen; it was his fear that Starfire could become a cog in the galactic-sized wheel that was *The Community*. He still wasn't sure if the organization was a force for good or evil.

"Please, Adam, let us explain," said Galena. She could see how concerned Adam was and dispensed with her jovial lightheartedness.

Adam sat down but on the edge of the seat.

"First of all," Galena began, "I have acquired only thirty-five percent of Starfire ownership. You still have your twenty-five percent, and Tidus retains thirty percent. The remaining ten percent will be made available for management incentives, including a new executive director and other top personnel. Tidus will still be the managing partner and will be free to pursue his political ambitions. It is to the company's benefit to have a powerful politician on the Board. The controlling coalition of you and Tidus, with your combined fifty-five percent of the shares, will be able to override my thirty-five percent share, even if I gain control of the other ten percent. You see, Adam, I do not want to run Starfire. I just want a piece of it."

Adam looked at Tidus. "And you're okay with this?"

"Galena is making a long-term, no-interest loan to cover all construction costs in exchange for her ownership share. I should say that is more than generous. Repayment will be simply a line item on the operating budget and will prove not to be a burden."

"Repayment is not a concern to me," Galena explained. Then she smirked. "It goes against my nature, but at one point, I told you that I would make this personal. I have been true to my word. It is now more important for me to make Starfire whole again than it is to make a tiny sliver of profit. I am sure you realize that the investment I am making in Starfire will barely register on my books. That is not bragging. That is simply a fact." Then she smiled. "And seeing that I now have a brain interface device, I am sure my fortunes will grow even greater going forward. Already, I am seeing the benefits of unfettered access to all the confidential records I need."

Then Galena leaned over and took Adam by the hand. "But I must say, this single gesture—that of helping you and Tidus—has brought me more pleasure and satisfaction than most of my other transactions of late. It feels good ... to do good."

Then she snarled playfully. "See what a bad influence you are on me, Adam Cain? I do not think I will ever be the same after meeting you."

"None of us are," said Tidus, also snarling but with a twinkle in his golden eyes. "He has that effect on people."

Adam felt his face turn beat red. He wasn't used to this kind of attention.

"So, what happens next?" he asked awkwardly.

Galena now reached over and took Tidus's hand, forming a circle between her, the Juirean and the Human. "Now we move forward, with new adventures and misadventures—"

"Oh, and one other thing," Tidus interrupted.

Adam and Galena looked at him, frowning.

"When do *I* get an ATD? I don't like the idea of the two of you *thinking* behind my back."

The End

COMING SOON...

Human for Hire #12
EARTH BLOOD

Coming Soon…

Get your copy today.

AUTHOR NOTES

Another Human for Hire story is in the can. I hope you enjoyed it.

This book is special for me—*my 70th book in my 70th year.*

When I started my writing journey almost thirteen years ago, this was exactly where I wanted to be at this time. Not really, but it sounds good. How could I possibly have thought I could write 70 books? Very few authors have ever written that many books. And most of my fans have read them all. And for that, I thank you!

In reality, when I started writing *The Human Chronicles* (the first series featuring Adam Cain), I saw it as going on for five books. As the early story developed, I could see certain events happening and figured I could complete the storyline by then. I did that, but then I realized there was still a lot of Adam's story to tell. *The Human Chronicles* turned into 29 books, followed by the nine books in *The Adam Cain Saga* and the six books in *The Human Chronicles Legacy Series*. And now, I'm up to 11 books in *Human For Hire*, also featuring Adam Cain.

Yeah, 55 books about Adam Cain. And to tell you the truth … he's still going strong!

As an author, I have a responsibility to my readers to make each book new and fresh. That's not always easy to do, but I do it by constantly asking myself, *"What would my readers like to see in the book?"* This isn't solely about the book as a whole but in *every* scene. I'm constantly thinking about you … my reader.

And why shouldn't I? I'm writing these books for *you*. They are entertainment, so they have to be entertaining … *to you*. (Are you detecting a theme here?) And the fact that it's been going on for 55 books tells you that people are still entertained by the antics of Adam Cain, the alien with an attitude. And as long as I can keep the storylines fresh and exciting, I will continue to write Adam Cain books.

Now, I'd like to change subjects … a little.

When I set out to write a book, the idea has to be large enough to carry me/you throughout an entire novel. It can't be a single topic or a single event. There have to be multiple storylines going on at the same time. And then there has to be twists and turns to keep you—my reader—interested. After 70 books, I believe I have learned my craft well enough for that to happen.

However, every idea I come up with isn't always big enough for a book. That's why I started a **YouTube** channel where I can publish short stories, and all in the *Humanity: Fu*k Yeah!* genre (HFY). They all show Humans as the badasses in the galaxy, either intentionally or not. Also, I try to include humor in every story, setting my channel apart from all the others. Oh, and I write all the stories myself, not using A.I. Ninety-nine percent of all the other HFY channels use A.I. for story generation, and if you've ever listened to any of these, you can tell it right away. A.I. has a certain tone to it, and the stories all seem to end the same way. Check some out, and you'll see what I mean.

But my channel is different. These are stories with real Human emotion and with the twists and turns as only a Human can write. They're also a lot of fun to do. I'm not only writing short stories, but I'm also producing short videos/movies at the same time.

I'm a creative, and I have been my whole life. Now, I not only get to write novels, but I also get to write short stories and make videos. To call me a happy camper is barely scratching the surface. I'm walking on air, having a creative overload!

So, please check out my YouTube channel at **The Human Chronicles HFY**. Watch some of the videos and then **subscribe** to the channel. That will really help me out.

And now, for the next Human for Hire book.

I wanted to do a book a month until the end of the year (2024), but that schedule is a little too ambitious. So, I'll be premiering a new book approximately every 45 days. But if you want more of my writing style, and in more bite-size bits, go to my YouTube channel.

And be looking for the next HFH book, **Earth Blood**, available now.

Okay, that's it for now. Thanks for reading *I Am Entropy*. And remember, if you keep reading, I'll keep writing. (And I want to keep writing!)

Tom Harris
July 2024

FACEBOOK GROUP

I'm inviting you to join my exclusive, secret, Super Fan Facebook Group appropriately called

Fans of T.R. Harris and
The Human Chronicles Saga

Just click on the link below, and you—yes, **YOU**—may become a character in one of my books. You may not last long, and you may end up being the villain, but at least you can point to your name in one of my books – and live forever! Maybe. If I decide to use your name. It's at my discretion.

trharrisfb.com

Contact the Author

Facebook
trharrisfb.com

Email
bytrharris@hotmail.com

Website:
bytrharris.com

YouTube:
The Human Chronicles HFY

NOVELS BY T.R. HARRIS

Technothrillers
The Methuselah Paradox
BuzzKill

Human for Hire Series
Human For Hire
Human for Hire 2 – Soldier of Fortune
Human for Hire (3) – Devil's Gate
Human for Hire (4) – Frontier Justice
Human for Hire (5) – Armies of the Sun
Human for Hire (6) – Sirius Cargo
Human for Hire (7) – Cellblock Orion
Human for Hire (8) – Starship Andromeda
Human for Hire (9) -- Operation Antares
Human for Hire (10) – Stellar Whirlwind
Human for Hire (11) -- I Am Entropy

Human for Hire (12) – Earth Blood
Human for Hire (13) – Capella Prime

The Human Chronicles Legacy Series
Raiders of the Shadow
War of Attrition
Secondary Protocol
Lifeforce
Battle Formation
Allied Command

The Human Chronicles Legacy Series Box Set

The Adam Cain Saga
The Dead Worlds
Empires
Battle Plan
Galactic Vortex
Dark Energy
Universal Law
The Formation Code
The Quantum Enigma
Children of the Aris
The Adam Cain Saga Box Set

The Human Chronicles Saga
The Fringe Worlds
Alien Assassin

The War of Pawns
The Tactics of Revenge
The Legend of Earth
Cain's Crusaders
The Apex Predator
A Galaxy to Conquer
The Masters of War
Prelude to War
The Unreachable Stars
When Earth Reigned Supreme
A Clash of Aliens
Battlelines
The Copernicus Deception
Scorched Earth
Alien Games
The Cain Legacy
The Andromeda Mission
Last Species Standing
Invasion Force
Force of Gravity
Mission Critical
The Lost Universe
The Immortal War
Destroyer of Worlds
Phantoms
Terminus Rising
The Last Aris

The Human Chronicles Box Set Series
Box Set #1 – Books 1-5 in the series
Box Set #2 – Books 6-10 in the series
Box Set #3 – Books 11-15 in the series
Box Set #4 – Books 16-20 in the series
Box Set #5—Books 21-25 in the series
Box Set #6—Books 26-29 in the series

REV Warriors Series
REV
REV: Renegades
REV: Rebirth
REV: Revolution
REV: Retribution
REV: Revelations
REV: Resolve
REV: Requiem
REV: Rebellion
REV: Resurrection

REV Warriors Box Set – The Complete Series – 10 Books

Jason King – Agent to the Stars Series
The Unity Stone Affair
The Mystery of the Galactic Lights
Jason King: Agent to the Stars Box Set

The Drone Wars Series

BuzzKill

In collaboration with Co-Author George Wier...
The Liberation Series
Captains Malicious

Available exclusively on **Amazon.com** _and_ **FREE** _to members of_ **Kindle Unlimited.**